Shaun Levin

*the last chapter.
You've encoura-
ged from
close to the start.
Thanks.
Love,
Shaun.
Feb 2004.*

Seven Sweet Things
a novella with recipes

Seven Sweet Things
a novella with recipes

Shaun Levin

Published by bluechrome publishing 2003

2 4 6 8 10 9 7 5 3 1

First published in Great Britain in 2003 by
bluechrome publishing
An Imprint of KMS Ltd
38 Tydeman Road,
Portishead, Bristol. BS20 7LS

www.bluechrome.co.uk
A CIP catalogue record for this book is available from the British Library

ISBN   0 9543796 3 2

Earlier versions of some of these chapters were published in *Best Gay
Erotica 2002*, *Quickies 2*, *Mind Caviar*, and *Tears in the Fence*.

thanks

to Robert, his name is in brother, for wild rice and New York, to Laura, my loyal sis, for mandelbrot and Paris, to Karen, my big sister, for ocean milk and her faith, to Oren "Jinj" Kenner for his chewy fruit cake and a rich and precious friendship, to Sharron Hass for her spare ribs and lessons on love, to Amalia Ziv, faggot extraordinnaire, for chocolate brownies, to Sue Boyd for our macrobiotic baby and for making so much possible, to Agnes Makasi for khubu mielies and mngqusho, nourishment to last a life-time, to Emily Hauser for chocolates and a book (twice, so far), to Reuben Lane for his company in nice places, to Cherry Smyth for soup and our writing group, to Jo Broadwood for Persian rhubarb syrup and reading on the sofa, to Anup Karia for Melati and being my best Jewish friend in exile, to Sarah Salway for her words and for being my Sugar-Mummy at Fortnums, to Barbara Dimmick for long walks through Rosslyn Glen and listening to Chekhov by the fireside, to Leslie Dunton-Downer for foie gras and cannibals, to Hawthornden Castle for that month of beauty, to Sarah LeFanu for saying just do it, to Geoff Dyer for saying that was a work of genius, to Eva Lewin for saying yes, to the Arvon Foundation and Ty Newydd for their generous bursaries, to Auntie Leah and Uncle Neville for random acts of kindness, to my mother for her pickled fish and her music, to my father for the sea and for his sense of wonder, to Jerry Hyde, Anthony Delgrado, Jim McSweeney, and the people in Julia's group.

Sensuality is a consequence of love.

Jean-Luc Godard, *Alphaville*

"Don't you realise that the truth
is quite the opposite of what he said?"
Plato, *The Symposium* (Trans. Christopher Gill)

Contents

Ye have heard that it was said by them of old time, Thou shalt not commit adultery

St Matthew 5:27

Introduction:
When My Love Went Back

Rum Glazed Chocolate and Coconut Cake

Introduction: *When My Love Went Back*

Last night, when my love went back to his girlfriend and I forgot how much he loves me and that I still love him, I comforted myself with the making of a rum-glazed chocolate and coconut cake. The house was quiet, the upstairs people still at work, the neighbour's children not back from the cinema yet. There was room for anguish and anger to become diffuse, to flow unhindered from the usual hubbub they cause inside my head, to hover like darkness on the face of the deep. For wasn't it the loneliness of chaos that led Him to creation?

First I cleared the work-surface. And while I cleared, I thought, as I have been thinking recently, about Plato. Towards the end of his *Symposium*, Diotima tells Socrates, as he sits at her feet, that Love is the son of Poverty and Resource. This, she tells him, is how Love came into being: Poverty, despairing she'd be stuck in a rut for the rest of her life, creeps up on Resource and fucks him in his sleep. As for me, to even out the barrenness that threatens to overwhelm me when my love is not here, I find ways to feel resourceful. Last night was not the first time; I've learnt to feed myself in his absence.

Six months on and we have our ritual: he leaves soon after sunset, I stay at home. Our love is a daytime love; there is none of night's secrecy when we're together. Nothing is in the dark, yet everything has a shadow. I have learnt to write at night since meeting him. I have come to like the night. For the quiet it offers, for the hushed calls of the outside. But last night I knew I would not be able to write: That constant state of need, and the swiftness with which beauty disappears - his in me and my own - both stifled out any utterance. So I turned elsewhere for creation. A cake that is as soothing to make as bread; I've made it often, it's ease acquired after years of selling it at craft markets and making it for the children at the nursery school where I worked as a cook all those years ago.

The is the alchemy bit. Take 200g of butter and cream it with two cups of sugar. Two teaspoons of vanilla essence and two large eggs. Then add two teaspoons of baking powder and, gradually, a cup of flour. Then comes the part that is always the righting of a wrong: to see the curdled liquid turn into a batter. Pour in half a cup of milk and keep stirring. Then sprinkle in the coconut, not too finely desiccated, just half a cup, and two-thirds of a cup of cocoa powder, which will darken as you mix it into the batter. And finally another cup of flour, another quarter cup of milk, and a quarter cup of rum. And stir until you have a smooth batter flecked with coconut.

It was at that point, having created something for myself, been generous to myself, that my love for him grew and my frustration and craving began to subside. And I thought: Now I remember why I love you. These were some of the reasons I came up with in the time it took for the cake to bake: I love you because you tell me I am beautiful; I love you because you touch me more tenderly than any other man ever has; I love you because you suck on my nipples like you trust me to heal you of the mother who gave you away for adoption; I love you because you tell me never to doubt myself; I love you because you say there are days you miss me so much you cry; I love you because you say you're not sure whether the look on your face when I fuck you is one of joy or sadness, and I wondered, as I drank my tea and waited for the cake to rise and set, whether you knew that that's what it felt like to be inside you.

There were dishes to wash: bowls and spoons from our lunch; plates and cutlery from other days. The kitchen had to be cleaned, the work surface cleared, before the cake could be taken from the oven, gently, and left to cool for a while as I mixed the rum with butter and sugar, and boiled it into a syrup. Then I brushed the glaze over the top of the cake. I could have had a slice soon after that, or kept it all for today, as I often do, keep the cake for the following day. For once I've created my cake, I am resourceful, hopeful; to remove a fragment would detract from the whole I need to hold onto for as long as I can. But then, I thought, it is better that one of the pieces be sacrificed, rather than my whole body be cast into the hell of your absence. So I took the knife and I cut the cake and I ate from it. And it was good.

Rum Glazed Chocolate and Coconut Cake

In a big mixing bowl cream 200g butter or margarine with 2 cups of sugar. Mix in 2 eggs, then 1 teaspoon salt and 2 teaspoons vanilla essence, and, slowly, 2 cups of self-raising flour, adding ¾ cup milk and ¼ cup of rum as you go along. Stir in ½ cup of desiccated coconut, and ½ cup of cocoa. Bake at gas mark 4 for 1 hour and 15 minutes. For the glaze, which is a later addition, for originally this cake was the birthday cake I made at the nursery school where I worked as a cook, and it was a great favourite; even after I left, parents would call and ask for this cake, sometimes insisting on bright green icing. So for the glaze: boil up ¼ cup of rum, ¼ cup of granulated sugar, and 25g of butter. Just a quick boil, until the sugar has dissolved and the butter melted; the mixture shouldn't be allowed to get too syrupy. Brush the glaze over the cake.

Later came

The Vegan Version

Cream 100g soya margarine with ¾ cup of granulated sugar, add 2 teaspoons vanilla essence, 2 teaspoons baking powder and 1 teaspoon bicarbonate of soda. Fold in 2 cups of flour and ½ cup of cocoa, alternating with 1 very full cup of soya milk. Bake at gas mark 5 for 40 minutes. I'm always surprised by the vegan fear of cocoa, as if cocoa were milk chocolate and carob the only alternative. I find carob offensive and overpowering, but that might have something to do with the first job I ever had when I was 15 and sent to work in a carob grove near Ashkelon, which is the place we left South Africa for. If you insist on carob, then use brown sugar instead of granulated sugar, otherwise it all gets too sweet.

What a Muse Looks Like

Scheherazade's Oatmeal Cookies

What A Muse Looks Like

I see my beloved in the body of Christ. I catch the blood that drips from his open palms; lick the flesh from around the stakes in his feet; adore his arms stretched out like wings, the sweet wisps of hair in his armpits, like one ostrich feather. And all in the perfect Florentine landscape. Wherever I look as I wander through The National Gallery, my love is there; every immaculate body his: seduced by Caravaggio to pose naked with grapes, watched over in his sleep by Botticelli to be transformed into Mars. He is sleek, muscular, baby-faced perfection; with his body close to mine, I rejoice in myself.

Today he brought bagels and I offered him carrot and coriander soup (the biscuits were cooling in the oven, the house filled with the smells of melting sugar and vanilla essence). My beloved is a cat; I know he'll stay with the one who feeds him the most. I am not his only love, you see; he is a hungry and confused man, devoted to many. It's another cool summer and I've gone back to soups: Tuscan bean; Moroccan spinach and chickpea; tomato, bread and basil.

"Am I allowed seconds?" he says, lifting his eyes from the bowl to smile at me.

"More?" I say.

"This soup is so good," he says. "You are such a good cook."

Let me kneel now and give thanks for kind words. Let me show you my gratitude as you bend over to offer yourself to me. We finish lunch and return to our island, our centre, our magnet, my futon in the middle of the bedroom, where my love lies on his back and purrs as I slide in and out of him, his muscles loosening until there is nothing left but devotion. This is my calling and my consolation. I am here to feed and fuck my beloved. We stare at each other, our eyes wide open, not speaking, the words hovering beyond the confines of passion where anger and history lurk.

"Say my name," he says.

"Why?" I say.

"Say it," he says. "I want to hear you say my name."

"Sweetheart," I say, stroking the insides of his thighs, his knees resting on my shoulders.

"My real name," he says, his open palms on my cheeks to make me stop.

"Martin," I say.

"Keep saying it," he says. "You live in a fantasy world."

My love is right. I have too much time on my hands, too many hours in the day to plan my next move, our next conversation, his farewell speech. I need something to keep me from loving him constantly; I need a break from all this. My love for him is a full time job. It's how I fill the days of the week when he's with her. And with another him, for all I know. So then, I think, if I fuck him harder, and slowly build up speed, and get deeper inside him, then he will no longer be able to extract me from his body.

"It's starting to hurt," he says.

"Is that a good or a bad thing?" I say.

"I don't know," he says, laughing, the lines that radiate from the corners of his eyes curving down to meet the ones arching up from his mouth; his face bracketed by its own grooves. This is where time manifests itself on his body, and in the tough dark hairs in his ears; except for that, his body is self-made and baby smooth, formed by hours at the gym, moulded into porcelain.

"I love feeling you inside me," he says.

"I love being inside you," I say.

"Do you?" he says.

"I want to be there always," I say.

I am going soft, but I stay there, my sweat dripping onto his chest, the beads rolling off his skin and onto the sheet. Nothing clings to my love.

"That feels so good," he says.

"Tell me I'm beautiful," I say.

"Why?" he says.

"Tell me," I say. "Tell me I'm beautiful."

"You're fucking beautiful," he says. "You're beautiful. You are."

"Again," I say, getting harder.

"You're beautiful," he says.

On the day we met, after we'd made love for six hours, I thought: So this is what a muse looks like. This is what Picasso relied on to keep painting. This is what Gertrude saw in Alice, what Lewis Carroll saw in his colleague's little daughter. I rely on every type of beauty to keep writing: the beauty of trees and rocks, mud and long walks through forests, kneeling by a stream to wash my face in icy water. I need to get close to creation to create. My love is creation; he is the chaos made perfect.

"Don't come yet," he says.

"I'm not," I say.

"Your eyes were glazing over," he says. "Tell me something."

"Like what?" I say, backing out of him, his arse grabbing at me just before I leave.

"Anything," he says, lifting his feet off my shoulders and easing them onto the bed.

My love draws me towards him, to lie on his chest, our lips brushing together.

"Please," I say. "No words yet."

"You never tell me things about yourself," he says.

"Should I get us some cookies from the oven?" I say,

kissing his lips.

"Is that all you're going to say?" he says.

"I'll get us tea and cookies," I say. "And *then* I'll tell you things."

In the kitchen, naked, the oven's left-over heat warm against my chest, then on my back, as I turn to set the baking tray down on the table, I wonder if it will ever be possible to give myself to him. To open up and be known. My beloved is right; I don't like talking about myself. I don't trust words, especially spoken ones, especially my own; they're a mask and a deceit. I prefer all interpretations of me to be based on what I do. And yet, if he looked closely at my actions, at the things I did while he's with her. If he could only imagine what it's like to be here while he's there, he'd know so much about me he'd want to be sick.

I count eight cookies and put them in a lapis lazuli ceramic bowl, from the set we'd eaten our soup out of, and place the rest of the cookies on the cooling rack. They are thin and crisp and warm from the oven. I take a bite from one on my way back to the bedroom. I want to make my entrance, chewing; to appear from behind the door like a lover returning from his travels, like Odysseus surprising Penelope, like Socrates coming in with a frown from the neighbour's patio, arriving late for Agathon's celebration dinner.

"What about me?" my love says, lifting his head from the pillow and resting on his elbows.

"I'm coming," I say. "Open wide."

I sit on his middle, his cock soft between my arsecheeks, and slot a whole cookie into his mouth. I'm Scheherazade feeding her emperor to keep him from chopping off her head. Why was he so afraid of sleep, so desperate to rely on the stories of others? My offerings are much more substantial than stories. Last week there was chocolate and coconut cake, today there are oatmeal cookies.

"Oh, my God," he says. "I love these biscuits. What's in them?"

"Guess," I say, taking another one for myself and putting the bowl on the floor by the bed.

"Okay, okay, don't tell me," he says, opening his mouth for another bite. "Raisins?" he says. "And cinnamon?"

I smile as if he's guessed my secret, rescued me from the awkwardness of self-revelation; he has named the parts of my inner world kept hidden out of shame and fear. I don't want this to stop. But he distinguishes between tastes; he spots the coconut, the flour and the butter, the demerara sugar. My love is both beautiful and naturally gifted.

"I'm surprised," I say. "I can never single out ingredients."

"You make the best biscuits," he says. "You are the best cook."

"Again," I say, lifting my bum off his middle to massage his cock beneath me.

"The best," he says.

"And again."

"The best."

And slowly I sit back down and guide his cock into me.

"More," he says.

"What more?" I say, leaning down to lick crumbs from the cleft between his pecs.

"More biscuit," he says.

"They're cookies," I say.

"No," he says, "They're biscuits," lifting his middle to push deeper into me, turning his head, just a fraction, a sidelong glance at the bowl on the carpet.

So I reach for a cookie to feed him.

Scheherazade's Oatmeal Cookies

For about 100 cookies, which don't take as long as you think they might. Well, they do take long, but they're not hard work, and they freeze and unfreeze well (and you can eat them frozen). Have a book handy while you're waiting for each batch to bake. Sandra Cisneros' *The House on Mango Street* is good company, so is Janet Frame's *The Lagoon and Other Stories*, or *The Essential Rumi*, which should, anyway, be taken everywhere. So: Cream 300g butter with 1½ cups brown sugar and 1½ cups granulated sugar, then stir in 3 eggs. Add 1½ teaspoons bicarbonate of soda, 3 teaspoons vanilla essence, and 1 teaspoon cinnamon. Fold in 2¼ cups flour, then mix in - with your hands is easiest - 4½ cups rolled oats and 1½ cups chopped raisins, which are best chopped on a marble surface or wooden board with flour sprinkled on top so they don't stick to the blade. Then add a cup of mixed chopped nuts (or even whole sunflower and pumpkin seeds). On a baking tray, place teaspoonfuls of the mixture about 1" apart, then flatten each mound with the back of a fork dipped in milk - this way the fork won't stick to the dough - then bake until golden brown at gas mark 5 for about 30 minutes. Let the cookies cool and harden on a wire rack. Another way of doing this is to roll the mixture into little balls, chocolate-truffle size; have a pile of them ready for baking, then all you need to do between chapters or poems is place and flatten the dough on the baking tray before putting each batch into the oven. Do two trays at once; one on a rack nearer the top, the other nearer the middle. One more thing: these cookies, which I think are the best, and the most comforting, and the least guilt-inducing, are great crumbled up with fresh yoghurt. They also appear in the recipe for Cheesecake Thingies on page 111.

But thou, when thou prayest, enter into thy closet.

St Matthew 6:6

The Outer Limits of My Aspirations

Cranberry, Raisin and Brandy Loaf

The Outer Limits of My Aspirations

"These are for you."

Handmade chocolates in a small white box bound with a thin lilac ribbon. I hand them to my love as we walk through Lincoln's Inn Fields, leaving Holborn behind us on our way to the river. Summer evening, and the air is damp with humidity and car fumes. We walk beside the railings through the fields smelling of wet grass and rust. The chocolates are soft; we eat one of each: Cointreau truffles, rum truffles, orange and walnut creams. My love keeps bumping into me, nudging my shoulder, looking at me as if over the top of spectacles, and laughing.

"You're in a giggly mood today," I say.

"I'm glad to see you," he says.

"I was almost late," I say.

And I make my love listen to the journey I took to get to him: There were no trains from Blackheath, where I'd been running a workshop all day, getting old people to record the details of their war years (almost all of them had been taken from their homes and sent to live in the countryside), so I got a cab to Lewisham, then a train to London Bridge; all the while feeling accompanied in the world, less fragile than usual, loved by a man, connected to him as I stood in a carriage on the Northern Line to Bank, then the Central Line to Holborn, and up the escalators, moving without having to move, then into the light, and there he is, my love, waiting beside the newsstand with a smile, a reduced version of one six times its size.

"I'm not going to kiss you," he says, as he leads me like a blind man down Kingsway. "People know me here."

"Do they?" I say. As if all this is news to me.

We're passing Sir John Soane's Museum; everything, my

love tells me, is as it was in Victorian times: the furniture, the crockery, the plumbing, everything that was this man's home has been left as it used to be. And there are Hogarths all over the place. At this time of day, though, it is closed, so we turn right and keep walking through the Law Courts and down towards the LSE, where my love lectures in mergers and acquisitions. We're still new to each other, eager to display the sceneries of our day-to-day existence. Pointing to the buildings covered in a film of carbon residue, my love tells me why Downing Street is painted black; the soot that has always coated the prime minister's house is what makes it recognisable to Londoners.

Ever so quickly, as he's engrossed in his own stories, a peck on his shoulder, a kiss before continuing on our way along the sidestreets of the LSE to Clement House on Aldwych where my love takes me down to the study-room in the basement. This is where he sits sometimes, pretending to read or work at a computer, just so he can feast on the Italian and American students who've come for the summer in their shorts, and their punk-rock and Greenpeace T-shirts. Now, at 5pm, the desks are unclaimed, the place is empty; our own sounds - stepping into the room, the heavy wooden doors closing behind us, our breathing - are all hushed by thick wooden tables, by the wall panelling, and the plush red carpets. Everything smells of rosewood. This is where our love began: on the day my love stepped out of the Bisexual chatroom and into London Bears to ask if I'd fuck him.

So much depends on a beginning, the story we carry with us for the ones who will ask: How did you meet? One must always be ready with an answer; people are eager to know and one must be enthusiastic in one's response. The need for an answer is the need for a tale about the beginning of love. If Eros was born with the blade of a sword piercing an ostrich egg afloat on the ocean, the story people want must be as dramatic as that. And by dramatic I mean romantic, and by romantic I mean fate's pivotal role in the birth of love. How many times did the sword come down before it hit the right egg?

"We don't have to whisper down here, you know," he says.

"I was enjoying the quiet," I say.

"They'll be here soon," he says.

"Who?"

"The noisy and the beautiful," he says.

"Take me to the toilet, then," I say, tugging on his sleeve.

"It's up those stairs there," he says, pointing.

"Take me," I say, pulling him with me.

So that we can hug. So that we can do the things he forbids us in public. So that he can rest his head on my shoulder and say, his face transformed by sadness and loss: "I think I am falling in love with you." That's what he says. He says: "Falling in love with you." Can I say it just one more time? "I think I'm falling in love with you." And again I am moved to silence, a silence born out of the knowledge that every wrong word has the power to dispel magic. I don't need to say anything; I know he means the three words he avoids by repeating, when we're naked in bed, how much he loves my chest, how he loves my skin. I love your touch, he says. I love feeling you on top of me, and against me, and inside me. My love can put everything after "I love," except "you." It has taken him this long to be just one preposition away from the three-worded monster. My love's courage manifests itself in other ways.

Don't talk to me about pride and dignity; I'll do anything to keep him by my side.

"Come," he says. "I'll show you a hidden treasure."

On our way to the Embankment Gardens we stop off at the Roman Bath in the basement of an old building, at the back of an unused tube station, there to be looked at through a dirty window pane. This is one of the archaeological puzzles of London. It's up to the visitor, the sign says, to believe whatever story he wishes: is this a relic of Roman London; or a bath built by the Arundels and the Norfolks; or is this where the Earl of Essex came to soothe his aching love for the Queen, in the pure waters from the spring on Holywell Street. We look through the grimy windows at a bath big enough for the two of us, our noses pressed against the cool glass, hoping for the smell of sulphur, a childhood smell from the warm springs in Aliwal North. A Japanese couple are going over the sign with a dictionary. A chef on his way home from work, navy blue gingham trousers, about to unbutton his stained white shirt, about to reveal his neck, passes us as we head down Strand Lane.

And here we are again: on a bench drinking tea from styrofoam cups and eating cake; this time, pre-packaged coconut flapjacks from a café off the Victoria Embankment. This is not a country where one can survive without tea for long. The heart needs constant warming; winter is never far away. Even now, at the height of summer, this month of August, at one time the beginning of spring when my love and I were boys on the tip of another continent, on the edge of another hemisphere, even now the cool evening air can stick to your skin like frost.

"Are you okay?" my love says. "Are you alright?"

"About what?" I say. "I'm fine."

"I don't know," he says. "About us. I want you to be okay about us, about you and me. Cause I'm okay, I'm okay about us, more so than I've been about anyone for a long time."

If only he knew. If only I were strong enough, brave enough, adventurous enough to tell him how much I adored him. If only I could let him know that every day with him is glory and gratitude. But I am a coward and I am a liar.

"Let me read to you," I say. "I want to read something nice to you."

I've been carrying *The Symposium* around with me for days, drawing comfort from the luxury of others. This is where I've been turning to for lessons on love. Now I want to show my beloved what I've learnt, what the outer limits of my aspirations look like. Let him see the parameters within which I'm operating. I'm not sure who I am in Plato's story. Sometimes I'd like to be Socrates, welcomed by all no matter how late I wander in for dinner, or Apollodorus, the one you run to for his version of events, his take on the great banquets and the enlightened conversations. I read to him from Phaedrus' words on his army of lovers; about the fear of acting disgracefully in front of your boyfriend, and about Orpheus' crime: being too spineless to die for the one he loved.

"You're such a romantic," my love says.

"Stop being so cynical," I say. "Love does inspire bravery."

"Love is fickle," he says. "And how old was this Phaedrus anyway?"

There's no point in talking about love to a lover. Look how terrified Pausanias was, waffling on about Heavenly Love, afraid his writer-boyfriend would run off with the aging Socrates. Does my love feel accused by the stories I read him, are they a spotlight on his infidelity and treachery? (Ah, yes, I think, but the elegance with which these stories are being told!) I have taken Phaedrus' words and made them my own, put them in a context that is not a group of men lounging around, sipping wine from golden goblets, and giving praise to love. It's just the two of us in my story, clinging to each other to ward off all doubt. *The Symposium*, like all great art, like the still life with oranges and walnuts, like Reni's painting of Lot that you keep going back to in the National Gallery, like the opera you fly off to La Scala to see for the third time, like the secret you've just been told, how delicious they all are for those hours that you can keep them to yourself.

"What do you like about the book?" my love says.

"That it's about love and culture and having time for both," I say.

"You just need a proper job," my love says.

"These guys never worried about a job," I say, putting the book back into my bag.

"Did the woman call you from the college?" he says.

"I'm not interested in me," I say. "Let's just talk about Alcibiades and Pausanias."

"How are you going to survive if you don't take that job?" he says.

"I'll bake," I say. "I'll get another stall at Spitalfields."

"Well, at least you'll make better cakes than this," he says, eating the last of his flapjack.

My love holds out his hand for my wrapper, and takes them both to the bin, and when he's gone, I think: Let it always be this way; to be able to see him when he gets up and leaves, to know where he is when he's not near my skin. This casual going away and an imminent return. His walk so elegant and unselfconscious; a bum so tight in his cream-coloured Levi's, how could one not want to live just to bury one's face between those arse-cheeks. A shirt that never creases, always tucked in, always tight against his perfect body. He even irons his Y-fronts. She dusts and hoovers.

They, too, rely on a series of tableaux vivant. And here the garden is in bloom. Purple, yellow, orange, red, all contained in green. Pansies and roses and big fat pink hydrangeas.

There's a child playing on a blanket on the lawn in front of us, his mother and father feeding him toys: a red and yellow pick-up truck for his brontosaurus rex; green, blue, and red plastic hoops which he wears as bangles; a duck made of wooden blocks. Two men on the grass behind me are talking. The first one says: "There's nothing worse than being bitter." So the other one says: "Does that mean you're bitter with him?" And the first one says: "Yeah." Like duh, isn't that obvious? The sky is still blue and the late-afternoon traffic along the Embankment is a background hum by the time my love comes back to sit with me, his fingers brushing against the fabric of my trousers, the surface of my skin alert as if we were naked in bed.

"So," he says. "Should I come to yours tomorrow?"

"That would be nice," I say.

"Are you sure you don't need to work?" he says.

Winding the lilac ribbon over and under my fingers, playing cat's cradle for one. This is the colour of chicory flowers before they turn pale at dusk. Summer evenings in the garden. The quiet and the birdsong that come at the end of day. The boy moves across the grass towards the flower bed, laughing at his parents' calls from their nest on the blanket - "Come back, Finn. Bring back the water, sweetheart" - giggling, that perfect response to insincere tenderness, as he empties the bottle of mineral water onto the row of primulas.

"I'll take the day off," I say. "We can have lunch together."

"And then?" he says.

"I made some cranberry and raisin loaf," I say.

"I'll need a cuddle first," he says.

"I'll cuddle you now," I say.

"Not here," he says.

"I'll put my arms around you now," I say.

"Will you be naked?" he says. "I love the feeling of your chest hair against me."

"I love the warmth of your tummy," I say.

"I love yours."

"I love running my fingers down your spine," I say.

"I love sucking your nipples," he says. "I love sucking them."

"I love it when you sit on my face," I say.

"That turns me on so much," he says. "Especially when you make those noises."

"I love being inside you," I say.

"Do you like that?" he says.

"What?"

"You know what," he says.

"Do you mean fucking you?" I say.

"Yes," he says.

"Will you fuck me one day?" I say.

"Maybe," he says.

"What do you mean 'maybe'?" I say.

"You give me so much," he says. "I want to give you something."

To disappear. Gone. Just like that. As if every opening of the legs were an offering and a benefaction. When Agathon spread his legs for Pausanias, his paranoid, cynical old queen of a lover, was he furnishing him with a gift? Did he close his eyes and imagine Socrates' cock going in and out of his bum-hole? Did Pausanias, while making love to his bright and beautiful star of a boyfriend, ask Agathon to tease his arse with a spit-wet finger, his way of remembering his first daddy-love? How does one go about teaching the beloved to become a perfect lover?

"I love being fucked by you," my love says.

"I think I feel a stirring in my groin," I say.

"You're bad," he says. "I've got to go; I've got students waiting."

"Lucky students," I say.

"Lucky me," he says, touching my shoulder.

"Can Katherine bake?" I say.

"Don't start," he says. "I'll see you tomorrow."

At Somerset House they're waiting for the treasures to arrive from the Hermitage in St Petersburg. The courtyard has been sealed off to build a fountain where once military tattoos were held, where Cromwell's wax effigy lay after they'd buried him in Westminster. The bus shelters on the Aldwych are crowded, businessmen going home, tourists looking for places to go now that the museums and the galleries are shut for the night, and my love - can beauty really be scared of anything? - is showing signs of edginess.

"Don't worry," I say, for we are approaching Clement House. "I'm not going to hug you."

"I don't want to argue either," he says.

"I said," I say. "I'm not going to hug you."

"Ah," he says.

"Interesting Freudian mis-hearing," I say.

"Yeah," he says. "Very interesting," laughing as he places an open palm on the back of my neck, his other hand pressing gently between my shoulder blades.

"Watch it," I say, all mock-anxiety. "People know me here."

"Stop it," he says. "I'll come round tomorrow."

And I'm left, a body choking and half-dead on the battlefield. Please God, get me out of here. Give me a reality grander than this aloneness, an existence of more than just abandonment, a context richer than having to take the Underground back to Finsbury Park, then the 106 to Stoke Newington. I want something bigger than a simple return journey home. So it's back down the Aldwych, past the chapel for the Navy, the one for the Airforce, along the Strand, looking between buildings for glimpses of the river. Every sophomoric face heading down Fleet Street is about to be tutored by my love. Faced with all this beauty, a man less perfect than him would be petrified.

Keeping him alive until I am there, at the top of Ludgate Hill, at St Paul's, where evensong is on the second lesson, Ahab and Obadiah, and then the hymn, which fills me like a requiem and enfolds me like a blanket. Let us bring thoughts of our sins to mind. Holy God, holy and strong, have mercy upon us; Jesus, Lamb of God, have mercy upon us; Father of all, have mercy upon us. Let us pray: We pray for the ministers in Palmer's Green and Pond's End; for little James' Uncle Paul and also his Uncle Peter, we pray they are happy in heaven; and now that the Olympic Games are coming to an end, we pray for all sportsmen and all sportswomen, and bless all games and those who play them. Through Jesus Christ our Lord.

Now take it, boy, and run.

I'll be Alcibiades, making my entrance, inebriated and adolescent, indifferent to the laughter of the other symposiads: I know I'm carrying the truth, and I know how gorgeous I am. Move over and make room; let me drape these pink and orange boa feathers around my love's perfect shoulders. How wonderful he looks with his toga casually draped around his waist. And while the slaves remove my sandals and massage my feet with wild violet oil, I'll be startled to hear your voices so close to me on the couch.

How near you're all sitting to my sweetheart. Let me pluck feathers from the boas around his neck, these apostrophes of pink and orange, and make them fall like snowflakes into your hair. Into yours and yours and yours.

And now, I'll say. Let me get you all as pissed as I am.

Cranberry, Raisin and Brandy Loaf

In a bowl, soak a cup of raisins in ¾ cup of brandy overnight. The next day: Cream 225g butter with 1½ cups of soft brown sugar. When the sugar looks like it's softening, add 4 large eggs, stirring them in one at a time. Add 2 teaspoons vanilla essence, ½ a teaspoon bicarbonate of soda, then fold in 3 full cups of self-raising flour, and finally 2 cups of fresh cranberries along with the raisins and the brandy they've been soaking in. Bake in two loaf tins lined with greaseproof paper at gas mark 4/180°C for an hour and 15 minutes. (These loaves freeze well.)

This cake started out as a

Banana and Sesame Loaf

Do the same as above until after the egg stage (no raisins, though, for this recipe), then add 2 teaspoons vanilla essence, 1 tablespoon desiccated coconut (optional), a ½ a teaspoon cinnamon (optional), and a little less than ½ a cup of sesame seeds. Fold in 3 full cups self-raising flour, and finally 5 large ripe mashed-up bananas. Bake as above.

My Let-There-Be

The Birth

My Let-There-Be

Before all that there was this. Once upon a time there was a girl flute-player and a boy fisherman who met and fell in love on a summer's day in the Twelfth Month. This story begins far away from here, in a land on the flip-side of the map. The flute-player was sitting with her sisters in their black Triumph on the beachfront, talking about the new Miles Davis record, about Dollar Brand who they'd seen in a night club in Cape Town, about the shortness of summer holidays, when the fisherman, in his black woollen cap and a beard he hadn't shaved all week, came up from the sea with the morning's catch. The fisherman's eyes were sad. He was still grieving for his young wife who'd died. She'd been known throughout the land for her beauty and her playfulness. As the fisherman got closer to their car window, the flute-player and her sisters put on their masks. And the fisherman fell in love.

My father was always silent and patient in his solitude, my mother performed in smoky bars after we'd gone to bed. I was conceived on the eve of Passover, *Erev Pesach* 1963, which is why I'm compelled to tell stories, to pass them on, to repeat myself, over and over again recounting the same story, always the same story, just in case I forget. It's not my job to keep coming up with new ones. The only thing that changes is the audience, the people who sit around the seder table, which of course is everything.

Nine months later and I'm pushing slowly through the birth tunnel to squelch out of my mother's cunt. No welcome could ever compensate for this gesture of rejection. No amount of cheering or smiles or smacks on my bloody arsecheeks could be a warm enough reception. I'm ready to turn around and go back home.

Now my love is my let-there-be; one word from him brings me out of the chaos or catapults me back again. Each word of his changes who I am, flings me from wall to wall; I can be four and fourteen and twenty four, within seconds. He is my mother and my father; he is either or both, I'm never sure. He is my talk and my song; every word and every silence with him is a memory altered.

"... gods as well as humans allow lovers every kind of indulgence."

Plato, *The Symposium*

Bumping Into People I Know

Phil's Lemon and Poppyseed Cake

Bumping Into People I Know

This is how we get ready to come today: like teenage boys, like perverts, jerking each other off, fists oiled with spit and ID Glide. You're nibbling on the tips of my nipples, my tongue up your backside; we are acrobats. Sometimes I think my joints will snap, that I'll rip my tongue from my mouth if I keep lapping at you the way I do. Sometimes I think you'll gnaw off the tips of my tits, your hunger like a memory too terrifying to articulate. And when you do, when we get to the point where you've had my blood on your lips, tasted that wheat-grain of flesh between your teeth, got over the shock of having my nerve-ends in your mouth, will you then be faithful to me?

"Okay," I say. "Now."

And your cum falls like holy water, like kind words and promises. Mine, I let go of reluctantly, a surprise when it lands any further than the edge of my pubic hair. In the year before we met, my shooting had dwindled to a dribble, and like other changes to my body - the grey hairs on my chest, the bald patch like a yarmulke on my head - I sensed my internal desolation making itself known on my flesh. The realisation had been slow and complete: I would no longer be hitting the wall behind my head. There'd be no more: Ow, that was my eye. No more: Fuck, you shoot big loads. No more pornographic expressions of wonder about anything. Now you have changed all this; your beauty and your love have got me firing again. What a relief to discover that not everything about the body is irreversible.

"You're my spark," I say.

"Come closer," you say, curling against the side of my body.

These are honeymoon days, November in the Year of the

Dragon. At moments like this I could ask you to marry me. And what a fine view it would be from the steps of Hackney Town Hall. For you, my love, I'd wear a suit; to make you mine I'd collude in the moulds of hetero-patriarchy; I'd spend my last pennies to stand face to face with you, and with this ring I thee. But that fear of disappointment keeps me from asking for the images inside your head, the fantasies of us that you create. Could they ever be as perfect as mine?

Your breathing is slow and deep, your cheek on your hand on my shoulder, to keep the hairs on my chest from tickling your nose. I draw cum trails on your smooth skin, like a slug crossing slate, my finger sliding up over your hip and towards your ribcage. The ease with which it travels; how accommodating the surface of your body is. My other hand nestles between your legs, in the moist warmth of sweat and cum and lubrication.

"I want to draw you," I say.

"Draw me?" you say. "I didn't know you painted."

"I don't," I say.

"You're being secretive again," you say, lying back, your hands on your stomach, frowning. "What else can you do that you haven't told me?"

"With words," I say, sitting cross-legged beside you. "I want to put you into words."

To capture the curves of your chest muscles; the way the shadow falls across the cleft between your pecs; the folds of skin on your tummy like tight pleats as you bend to take off your trousers just after you get here; the delicate hairs in your armpit; the pencil marks of those around your arsehole; your baby's, lint-free belly-button; your lips that carry memories of an ancestor who might have been black, like your penis and your nipples, brown-purple, several shades darker than your skin.

I want to imagine you before muscles covered your body. To put into words the parts that have remained unchanged by all those hours on the rugby field, in the swimming pool, at the gym. Hours spent on hiding the essence, growing fruit around the pip. Ripening flesh to be eaten. These are some of the parts that cannot be changed: the feet, the cock, the balls, the arsehole, the spine, the nipples, the hair; all the rest is --

"Do you think armour and *amour* come from the same root?" I say, making casual conversation as I copy your body onto the page.

"Have you finished yet?" you say. "I don't like being looked at like this."

"Love as a suit of armour," I say.

"Whatever," you say. "Are you done now?"

"Should we go for a walk?" I say, as if I'm about to put my notebook down.

"We can have tea and cake in the park," you say.

Your head is on my thigh. I kiss your forehead, your eyes rolling back to meet mine. I am a Buddhist monk with a treasure in my lap. My bowl of rice. I can let go of my pen now and feast.

"Maybe I've got some cake here," I say.

Last Saturday, after lunch at the Kurdish Restaurant on Kingsland Road, we lay on the sofa, me propped up against the arm-rest, your back against my front, and I read to you from *Joseph and the Old Man* - the story of two lovers who write books in the same room in a house on the beach, each looking out of a different window at the sea - until you fell asleep, your snores as invaluable as a secret. Now I keep trying to ease you back into sleep with words or lovemaking.

"You know there's always cake here," I say.

"I didn't want to sound greedy."

"If you don't ask," I say. "You'll never know."

"What kind of cake?" you say, as you lift your arms over your head to flick my nipples with your fingertips.

"I think I might be falling in love with you," I say.

It's true: Jumping off the edge of a chasm doesn't kill you.

"Can we go now?" you say.

I put four squares of lemon and poppyseed cake and two white serviettes in a paper bag, which I carry like a Gucci purse, along with my imaginary French poodle, a brother to Gertrude's Basket, prancing along Church Street on our way to Clissold Park. I make eye-contact, I smile, I say hello to strangers. God, am I happy. The government should be paying us to be in love. We're good for the neighbourhood. We lift the morale to heights heretofore unknown. The smells of our lovemaking trail behind us like maypole ribbons. And I know you're enjoying yourself; I know you are, just in a much more reserved fashion.

"Stop it," you say. "I'm not going to hold your hand."

"This is Hackney," I say, and I ruffle your hair, and pinch your cheek. "We're in the majority."

"Yeah, right," you say. "In your head."

I tell you that I'm always bumping into people I know, that I used to work in The Cooler, where half the neighbourhood buys its salamis and olives and ciabatta bread. I warn you that I know half the people around here. Though by the time we get to the park - having browsed in the shoe shop, looked at the menu in the window of Barracuda, stopped off at the library to renew my books - we still haven't bumped into anyone. We will, though, at some point.

At the cafe in the park in the old Manor House we stand in line for tea. Behind us, a mother clutches a four-foot tall Winnie the Pooh doll; her daughter holds onto Pooh's paw.

The girl has decided: She's not having ice-cream, she wants a drink.

"Is that orange juice or Ribena, Georgina?" her mother says.

While we wait, you look out the door at the men playing chess on the grass. When we're out in the world you stare at other men, allowing yourself the joys you abstain from when you're with her. When we're out in the world you become a great big bloody poof, and I am a narrow-minded, envy-riddled middle-aged man, possessive of the beauty I have stolen. You see, you are my one and only; to you, I am one of many.

I will make my questions ring effortless.

"What's out there?" I say.

"Just people," you say. "I love looking at people. They fascinate me."

"Yes," I say.

It is autumn and the leaves are changing colour; soon they will start to fall, even the slightest breeze will pluck them from their branches. It is one of those crisp blue days that make the world feel pure, that make being here a dream of escape. We walk to the pond with our styrofoam cups, and our paper bag of lemon and poppyseed squares, and in some strange way I realise that my life has changed. I have yielded, in my own staccato fashion, to the joy of connectedness. A group of teenage boys are doing chin-ups on the branch of a birch tree; further down the path two youngsters are kicking a soccer ball into a line of horse-chestnut trees, watching the pods fall to the ground and split open, then collecting the conkers into their pockets.

"I feel beautiful when I'm with you," I say.

"You are beautiful," you say.

I have tutored you well. Tell me nice things, I said to you

soon after we met; I've an entire childhood to make up for.

"Are you okay today?" you say.

"Am I being too much?" I say.

"I can handle anything," you say.

"Even 'I love you'?" I say.

"Those are strong words," you say. "Don't say them if you don't mean them."

"I won't."

"Still," you say. "It's a nice thing to hear."

Past the yew tree and the One O'clock Club, where the lawn is lush green, mothers and fathers standing with toddlers in their arms, clinging, reassuring themselves they can handle being alone at home with their babies. How difficult it must be for a mother to keep holding her baby when she's on her own. A black squirrel crosses our path, one of the last to survive from the dozens the council brought in from Japan last year.

There are ducks and coots; there are bulrushes on the banks and algae floating on the water's surface; there is a father and a son watching a labrador circling the inside of the fence that skirts the pond. Last winter I was here with a man who taught me the names of birds, though the only one that stuck was coot, because of the way its head moved, as if coot were a verb, the word for what it did. All that effort it made to swim without webbed feet. The pond was frozen then, and we'd looked for a stone to throw onto the ice to check how thick it was. I remember the ducks walking across the water, their turquoise-green heads catching the light like velvet, cobalt blue on their tails, and then, as we stood at the fence holding hands, I remember how they lifted themselves off the solid pond to fly upright for a while, then land back on their feet, webbed and bright orange. We couldn't find a stone anywhere.

"There used to be a shelter here," I say to you as we sit on a bench near the water. "I got a blowjob here one afternoon when it was raining."

"I love London when it's raining," you say. "Did you know the guy?"

"Not for long," I say.

"Did you fuck him?" you say, taking your slice of cake from the bag.

"I did," I say. "After the blowjob."

"Out here in the open?"

"Under the shelter, yes," I say. "With a curtain of rain around us."

"What happened to the shelter, then?" you say, preparing for your second mouthful.

"It burnt down," I say. "I think the dog's trying to get out."

"Mm," you say, your hand on your lips. Your delicate gestures; the way you lift the tips of your fingers to your mouth as if every crumb were the harbinger of an outpouring. As if your pleasure might brim over and spill down the sides of your face.

"The dog's stuck," you say.

"He can't get back onto this side of the fence," I say.

"How did he get in, then?" you say.

"They're not doing anything to help," I say.

The labrador walks along the inside of the fence. The son follows him, trying to find a way out.

"Did I ever tell you my goldfish story?" you say.

"You did," I say.

"Did you know the exact same thing happened to Jeffrey Dahmer," you say. "He gave his teacher a goldfish bowl with a goldfish in it and she gave it to his worst enemy, some little boy who put the bowl in his living room window for everyone to see."

"I wonder how the teacher felt when she heard what Jeffrey was up to," I say.

"I wonder why I didn't turn out to be a monster," you say.

"Because your mother held you."

"I know she did," you say, as if you'd never entertained another truth.

"The dog's struggling," I say. "Maybe we should lift it out."

"It's wet and dirty," you say. "And I'm wearing cream trousers."

"I'll do it, then," I say.

But I don't, because you're stronger than me, and you climb over the fence and talk softly to the dog, reassuring him that you're not going to hurt him, that you're there to help, and I'm a) envious not to be saving the dog, and b) saddened that you, sweet man, are not mine to keep.

"My hero," I say.

"I know," you say.

And the dog runs off as if it has somewhere to go, like a child running into a field knowing its father is close behind. Then he turns and sees he's on his own, no-one following him, so he skips around on the spot, playfully, as if unaffected by this lack of destination or master, and we look away, you and I, diverting our gaze so as not to embarrass the dog, and to make sure he doesn't come running back to us.

"My hands stink of dog fur," you say. "You'll have to feed me now."

And while I hand-feed you, a plane crashes on the runway in Paris, an earthquake reduces Izmit to rubble, and York is up to its waist in water. A man I know, a friend of a neighbour, is beaten up on Hackney Downs, and while one of his assailants kicks him in the ribs, the others circle him, their fists in their armpits, their elbows beating the sides of their bodies as if they were wings, singing cock-a-doodle-doo. The time is 4pm on a crisp cold bright November day. Any minute now Jack Straw's going to force the Lords to pass the Bill. Legal pubescent pricks are about to be loosed upon the world.

"When do you get back?" you say.

"On Friday," I say. "It'll be less than a whole week."

"What's there to do in Yorkshire anyway?" you say.

"Think," I say.

"You think too much," you say. "This cake is excellent."

"Open wide," I say, which is when I see them, out of the corner of my eye: the girls. They're always on time.

"Hey, love-birds."

"Hey," I say, getting up to hug them.

Ruth and Melissa in the park.

"This," I say. "Is Martin."

Everyone shakes hands, you in particular, like a visiting dignitary. You'd heard me mention them; they, on the other hand, knew everything there was to know about you: your girlfriend, my obsession with you, every single one of our positions. They have seen my cry on those days when I thought the shock of good things would kill me.

"What are you doing out?" I say. "Did you finish your essay?"

So we walk around the park, and Melissa tells you about *The Story of O*; Ruth and I a few feet in front of you, her hand inside my elbow, wondering if you'd picked up that everything was premeditated, a ploy to bring you out into the open of my world.

"I feel bad," I say.

"You'll get over it," Ruth says.

"I'm going to have to tell him," I say.

"What's this honesty fetish of yours?" Ruth says. "You're in love, for fuck's sake, not on *Oprah*. It's not his job to listen to your confessions."

"Did I tell you...?"

"Have you been eating cake again?" she says, her finger-tips on the side of my mouth.

"Lemon and poppyseed," I say.

"And?" she says, unhooking her hand from my elbow.

"I'll bring you some next time," I say.

"Some?" she says. "Now you'll have to make me those cheesecake thingies."

"I promise," I say. "I will. When I get back from Yorkshire."

It's getting dark and they're ringing the closing-time bell. You catch up with us to say you'd better be off; you want to be home in time for dinner, it's your turn to cook. So we walk with you to the gate. You head up Green Lanes, and the three of us walk back through the park towards Church Street, turning only once to wave, but by then you are out of sight.

Phil's Lemon and Poppyseed Cake

For a nice big tray cake, or two loaf cakes, which is how my friend Phil makes them, and then drenches them in lemon syrup, cream 275g butter with 1¼ cups sugar and 2½ teaspoons vanilla. Then add 5 large eggs and ½ a teaspoon baking powder, ¼ teaspoon salt, 2 tablespoons lemon zest, 5 tablespoons poppy seeds, and 3 crushed fresh basil leaves. I think it's easiest to add the bits and pieces before you start with the flour, because then they're in and they get evenly distributed. Add 2½ cups self-raising flour and about 5 tablespoons lemon juice. Bake at gas mark 5 for an hour.

Let the cake cool for about 10 minutes before you start making the glaze. For the glaze, melt ¼ cup granulated sugar, the juice of one lemon, and just under ½ a cup tequila or rum or Southern Comfort; any one will do! Bring this to the boil for a few seconds. Prick the cake all over with a skewer, then brush it with the glaze. This cake gets better as each day goes by; by day three it is perfect.

Lighter than a Drop of Rain

A Week in Yorkshire

Lighter than a Drop of Rain

MONDAY

Yesterday - last minute, I know - I called Katherine to see if she'd come with me again.

"You'll have enough women there with you," she said. "Take men."

"But I always take men," I said. "Last year with you was the best."

"I can't," she said. "I'm sorry," and coughed, pausing to spit blood into her hankie. "You see," she said. "That's why."

On the 11:58 to Leeds, a man in a pastel pink shirt and white cotton trousers pokes my shoulder.

"The seat you're sitting in is reserved, you know," he says.

"I know," I say, moving with my chicken salad baguette to sit by the window.

He doesn't seem to have any luggage, and when he sits down, the smell of him - coconut oil and washing powder - brushes against me like white sheets drying in the sun.

"I'm Socrates," he says. "And I'm not sure what the fuck I'm doing here."

He takes from his inside pocket a tub of Philadelphia cheese and some celery sticks.

"You're here for inspiration," I say, not missing a beat, licking mustard off my top lip.

"You need to stop holding onto the past as your only tense," he says.

"What?" I say.

The man behind us is talking to his bank; he's trying to track down the cheque to his therapist that has gone astray.

"Promise to be always in the present," Socrates says.

"Notice and reflect on things in relation to the present and the future. I'll keep reminding you about that."

The sun is out in Hebden Bridge as we walk through the woods to the house, then down to the river. Socrates is dawdling. I reach the river before him and squat by a small waterfall that crashes out all other sounds and keeps my thoughts from soaring into the metaphysical. It is only in complete silence that I remember who I am; in complete silence I can create.

"I need to hear water on stones," I say.

We've walked through the mulch and the bramble bushes to get to the stream where we wash our faces in the cool, brown water.

"Don't cry," Socrates says. "Beauty isn't a torment. Wrap yourself in it."

"But beauty weighs on me like the threat of abandonment," I say.

"No-one can remember that far back," he says, combing water through his hair.

"I was there," I say. "The serpent tried to tempt me first."

"Tell me more about water," Socrates says.

"It's soothing," I say.

"Because of your father?" he says.

"My father always made sure we were close to water," I say. "That's why he took us to Ashkelon, and before that to Vlissingen, Antibes, Viareggio, Pisa, and Venice. That's why he took us fishing. That's why we spent those dreaded summers at Cape St Francis. That's why, when cancer cells were chewing on his bones, when his vertebrae were collapsing in on themselves and grinding against each other, I swam with him in a cool stream for hours and hours, telling him how deep the water was, how cool it was on his skin, how it felt when he pulled his arms through it. And although he couldn't sleep, he rested, and held my hand for as long as I could keep us swimming.

"'Hold my hand, pops,' I'd said. 'Hold my hand.'"

"Is this going to be another cancer and death sob-story?" Socrates says.

"I wasn't intending it to be," I say. "I so don't want to start with sadness."

"Could you do a little bit on love?" he says.

"Not with my love so far from my skin," I say. "I rely on the body's proximity to keep me vital. And his is in Clapham."

"You need to love more," Socrates says. "You're putting all your eggs in one basket."

"But disappointment and longing are a grindstone around my neck," I say. "And I'm too weak to keep walking, if by walking you mean anything more than moving a pen across a page."

TUESDAY

Eighteen months today since my father's eyes shot open, phlegm dribbled from the side of his mouth, and his spirit sneaked out the bathroom window as I sat by his bed writing in my journal, the journal that is now a comfort when I'm away from my love.

Socrates and I sit by the window in the library, the only place in the house to escape breakfast-talk with strangers.

"Every man believes he has a great possibility," says Socrates.

This is what I want to know: "How do you find the

courage to do everything on your own terms?"

"It's solitude," Socrates says. "And drinking water out of a wooden bowl."

"I need wine," I say. "Wine and a big fucking spliff."

"Stop mucking about," Socrates says, getting up from his armchair. "Do you want to be a poet or not?"

"I want to write like a poet," I say. "But I'm too greedy to settle for so few words. I've been silenced for so long I couldn't just settle for a column of words; I need pagesful."

"I'll get us some scones," Socrates says. "Then we'll go for a walk."

When he gets back from the kitchen we leave through the dining room door. We walk down across the garden and back into the woods, his hand in mine, warm and dry. Our scones are in his rucksack; scones, a dictaphone, and a blanket.

"I can hear the water again," I say.

"We're going to drink from the spring," he says. "We'll be tipsy with water."

"Inspired by the air," I say.

"And charmed by the sunlight," he says.

"I'm so glad I met you."

"Come," he says. "Let's seek wisdom in the lovely waste of the woods."

"Nothing great was ever achieved without enthusiasm," Socrates says.

"By enthusiasm," I say. "Do you mean madness?"

"And by madness," he says. "Do you mean genius?"

We are lying on the blanket by the river. The robin's song is sharp, like sucked-in air. Red-faced midges settle on my knee. Red is the colour of change, and death.

Socrates' hair is wet from the stream, the drops of water

on his chest are smooth diamonds. I fold my clothes into a pillow.

"You're a genius," I say. "And you're mad."

"At least I'm enthusiastic," he says. "And I don't mind talking to the gods."

"What's the hardest task in the world?" I say, lying on my back, my hands behind my head.

"Don't distract me like that," he says, throwing his shirt over my middle. "The hardest thing is to think. To roam with a candle in the attic and ransack whatever's there. We're all wise; it just takes a while to discover how rich we are. We're all a version of the hundred volumes of Universal History."

"Can we have our scones now?" I say.

Lift them, I say. Lift them like the angels take the dead into heaven. Lift them like the mother lifts her baby son from the sand-pit to take him home for dinner, a dinner which is her. Lift these stories so that they feed and consume you, so that they carry you and act as your stepping-stones.

After dinner, Socrates and I walk away from the house towards the road. In the pitch dark the driveway is marked only by the shadows of the trees.

"I can't go far," he says. "My legs are tired."

"We'll walk as much as you like," I say, our shoulders touching as we make our way along the path.

I need this walk in the darkness to know where I am, to remember the place through its sounds and smells. The river in the distance, washing over moss-covered rocks, the damp grass, the wet earth. Socrates is silent, in one of his thinking moods; he doesn't trust small talk, for which I'm grateful, its subtexts are too unreliable and too demanding.

"How are you doing?" I ask him.

"Maybe just a bit more," he says.
"Up to the lights?" I say.
"Yes," he says. "It's easier doing the uphill bit first."

My wings are a swan's, their span the frame Dedaelus built to which he waxed every kind of feather from pigeon to peacock. Icarus' story is a warning to me, so I stay put, sorting out my feathers, keeping the wax far from the sun, long after my father has died.

"Come to bed with me," I say. "It's late."
    "In a minute," he says. "Let's have more tea. Maybe they've left some scones in the kitchen. I could show you the draft for my essay on Art."
    "It's bedtime," I say.
    "I'm warning you, though," he says. "I have to get up at seven tomorrow."
    "Well," I say. "We don't have to fuck, then."

WEDNESDAY
That autumn, when Patrick was visiting from Australia, we spent our mornings walking in parks - Regents, St James, and Finsbury Park, where Manoli has a cousin who lives above a Moroccan bakery on Seven Sisters Road. In the afternoons we'd hunt for bargain books before going off to the theatre or to Ronnie Scott's. That year Barney Kessel was in London and we'd taken him home, just as my mother and father had done twenty years ago in Port Elizabeth. It was on a Saturday, the day before Patrick and Manoli were to fly back to Australia, that Patrick and I spotted Katherine signing books in Waterstone's on Charing Cross Road. Patrick had met her at the Adelaide Festival some years back, and the three of us went for dinner at The Ivy.

Katherine was coughing a lot, every now and again spitting bloodied phlegm into paper serviettes which she kept in her jacket pocket. She said: "Writing is like a child; it needs all the encouragement it can get. Especially in its coming-into-being stages. Love your writing. Love the act of writing. Love the craft and the hardships and the sheer fucking joy of writing. Don't expect encouragement; you're not the child. Don't expect anyone to tell you what's right and wrong, because a) you're the one living with the child, and b) no one can know about your terror-filled childhood and what you're passing on to your creations."

"My god," said Patrick. "Lighten up, Kit."

Katherine ordered the salmon with the green beans and olives. Patrick and I ate the aubergine parmeggiano. We shared a bottle of red wine before going off to meet Manoli on Old Compton Street where Katherine met a young woman from Dalston and took her back to her hotel in Bloomsbury.

Food should be an occasion - a performance - a beautifully-wrapped gift - well thought out - expensive - unique - bought from a small shop on a side street in Mayfair or smuggled in from Tehran. Food should be a celebration - it should make people happy - feel special - a little embarrassed. Helpings should always be large - and like presents, there should always be more than one.

Don't tell your stories to everyone. If you have to repeat a story, make sure the ones who've heard it are out of the room, on the patio, hanging out at the other end of the marketplace. If you tell a story to a friend, who later hears you telling it to someone else, he'll feel betrayed; your gift to him will revert from gold back to ashes. Just think how deprived you feel when you catch Socrates sharing his wise bits with others.

"I heard that," Socrates says, coming into the library, his sandals in his hands.

"Those flowers look pretty around your neck," I say.

"The garden's beautiful at this time of night," he says

He sits by the bay window, reclining on the cushions, his robe exposing more than one might wish to see in a 63 year old man. I've seen it all, though, and I've kissed it, and I love him.

The *Qur'an* says: "We are all returning."

THURSDAY

Her dog was choking at the bottom of the hill. I was on my way down, running towards the level gravel road, picking up speed as I got closer, the sweat only now beginning to cover my skin. She was standing over her dog as I passed, the hem of her dress in the mud, talking to him in a tone one might use to coax a lethal weapon from the hands of a child: Cough it up, she was saying. Cough it up, Patsie.

And then: "Excuse me," she called, and I stopped. "Excuse me," she said. "Do you know anything about choking dogs?"

"What's he choking on?" I said, bending down to put my hands under his ribs.

"It's a squirrel," she said. "There's a squirrel bone stuck in his throat."

I lifted the dog, a weimaraner, onto its hind legs and leaned its back against my chest, then pulled up into its ribcage. It coughed up a lump of furry squirrel flesh, looked at me in surprise, and bounded off up the driveway back into the house.

"You must let me make you some tea," she said.

"I'll finish my run," I said. "Then I'll come back later, if that's okay."

"You run along," she said. "I'll see you at four."

"I look forward to it," I said.

"I'm Katherine," she said. "By the way."

Later, after lunch, the winter sun warm in a blue sky, I sit outside on the concrete slabs in the garden reading Rabindranath Tagore's *I Won't Let You Go*, afraid and longing to find the line we'd carved onto my father's tombstone. A drop of rain falls onto my hand. There is a tiny feather beneath it. This is a feather, lighter than a drop of rain.

I want to be excited by my own story. I want everything about me to be, like: Wow! I want to translate the details of my life into unforgettable tales of wonder.

"You said you like to tell lies about yourself," Socrates says.

"That was a lie," I say.

"Was it?" he says.

"Of course it was," I say. "And why's the library so dark anyway. I can hardly see myself think."

"Come sit here," he says. "Let me tell you something."

Socrates is almost invisible in the armchair, the green of his trousers and jumper blend in with the fern-green of the upholstery. I sit on the floor and lean against the armrest and feel the side of his knee against my shoulder. I want to say to him: Rest your hand on the top of my head when you tell me a story. And so he begins: "Once upon a time there were just the two of us, on a mountain, overlooking the valley."

Itself

Chocolate Coconut Fudge Bars

Itself

When I come back to London from up North, my love asks to be taught. He says: "I want to know, for when you go away again, how to make sweet things for myself. Teach me the sweetest thing of all." So I take him to the kitchen to learn.

"Okay, okay," I say. "Break the chocolate into cubes, then lay them out on the baking tray."

"And then?" he says.

"Melt the chocolate," I say, pointing to the cooker, where he crouches before the oven door, and prizes it open to slide in the baking tray.

"You wore that shirt when we met," I say. "I like that blue."

"It's purple," he says. "Look."

My love closes the oven door and turns to face me, holding up the hem of his shirt, which is all he is wearing. My love in a blue cotton shirt, the man I almost missed because he said purple and I saw blue. I'd arrived, as promised, in my grey jumper and khaki trousers, the first combination that came to mind when we spoke on the phone and I'd thought about this ballet dancer I'd picked up in a bar who'd said, on the way home, upstairs on the 73, "those colours look great on you." And this only days before my love and I were circling each other outside Finsbury Park Station, standing feet apart, leaning against a wall, looking at our watches, until I went up to him with the question - "Are you Martin?" - the question that has brought us to this moment: Me at the kitchen table showing him how to make chocolate coconut fudge bars; him showing me the colour of his shirt.

"See," he says. "Purple."

"Come closer," I say.

"Why?"

"It's dangerous to cook with your thingie out like that," I say. "Let me hold it."

Drawing his flat belly to my forehead, I rest against his soft warm skin, and move down to kiss the root of his cock, its head wrapped in foreskin, his balls small and delicate, his pubic hair so sparse at first I thought he trimmed it.

My love bends down to kiss me, as we'd bent to kiss Great-aunt Finnie, at 87, when we got back from Kol Nidrei on Yom Kippur, and she'd be in the kitchen grating carrots for the breaking of the fast. Our lips on cold, wrinkled skin. And now: as if my love and I must still be cautious with each other. Like strangers again after seven days apart, our tongues linger in each other's mouths like water snakes. Because that kiss was different. The way his mouth fitted against mine, like there'd been someone else since our last kiss. And why shouldn't there be? It only takes one kiss to change the way our mouths open for others. So I must kiss him more, get his mouth back to the shape that fits perfectly against mine.

"How's Katherine?" I say, pointing to the oven.

"Oh, shit," he says. "I forgot about the chocolate," and takes the tray from the oven, his bare bum facing me. "I told her about you,"

"Told her?" I say.

With the back of a spoon, my love spreads the melted chocolate over the base of the tray, and I get up to take the apron from the hook on the door, stand behind him, and wrap it around his waist. To shine his armour for him, sharpen his sword, brasso his helmet. It's the ones who stay behind at wartime who civilise the world.

"So what did you tell her?" I say, tying the knot.

"I said you'd just started lecturing at the LSE," he says.

"Why did you say that?"

"Because I miss you," he says. "I want to talk to people about you."

Leaning forward onto his back, my palms at his sides, I caress circles across his thighs, the softness of hairless skin pulled taut across muscle: a recurring wonder. The smell of chocolate takes me back to the Cadbury's factory in Port Elizabeth, driving past in the mornings on our way to school. Driving into the valley at the foot of Westbourne Road, and there by the stream, walls as high as chimneys, the smell that was the death of Augustus Gloop.

And years later, not long ago, sitting in Paris with Simon, only days before his illness took a turn for the worse and he died at the Mildmay just as we were about to fall in love. In Paris, then, sitting together at Deux Magots, him putting his nose to his cappuccino and looking up at me to say: "Do you think if I come back I could come back as the smell of chocolate?"

"Chocolate makes me sad," I say, my arms around my love's chest.

"What makes you sad?" my love says.

"Chocolate," I say.

"You're full of shit," he says, swaying his body back with mine.

"And you've got a great bum," I say.

"It doesn't feel that great," he says. "After what you've been doing to it."

Slamming. Growling. Whacking. Loosening my love's insides until there's no resistance. He's addicted to all this fucking, and what else can I do but feed his habit? So I kneel behind him and spread his cheeks to lap wet strokes across his arsehole with the flat of my tongue, like a dog licking sweetness from the palm of a hand. This is the taste of our lovemaking. My love steadies himself, his hands on the sides of the cooker, as he pushes back onto my face. If holes were big enough, if this little orifice at the core of our being was big enough, wouldn't we all be making our way back from time to time into the ones we adore? I wonder: If Zeus hadn't ordered Apollo to move the genitals to the front, would I not at this very moment be lapping at the warm sweet juices of my love's cunt?

"That feels nice," he says. "Where did you learn to do all these things?"

"From fantasy and desire," I say, standing up, a finger still in the wetness I've created.

"Why are your answers always so vague?" he says.

"Nicholas taught me to rim," I say. "In the house that we shared with the lesbians," as I take the tray to the fridge to let the chocolate cool, "Alex taught me to suck cock in his bedroom in Camberwell in front of the telly," and get the butter from the fridge, "Noah taught me to fuck when he'd bring his baker friend for threesomes," then the coconut from the cupboard, "David taught me to chew on nipples by nibbling on mine, the way Alex's wife had taught him to suck cock with her regular blowjobs," and then the caster sugar from the shelf, "Simon showed me things like licking between toes," and back to the fridge for the glacé cherries, "and how to gnaw on the lymph glands in the hollow of an armpit," and finally one small egg.

"See," my love says. "You can give a proper answer."

"Okay," I say. "Put the butter now in the saucepan."

Back in my chair at the breakfast table, cutting up cherries, I watch my love melt butter, to which he'll add coconut and sugar. Is this what we live for? - never mind fall in love for (just a vowel separating the two: love and live) - the wonder of watching a lover pour coconut, then sugar, from a white mug into a white saucepan on a day that could be spring, what with the sun shining like it is, barging into the kitchen window and flinging its arms wide open.

A few weeks ago we'd been talking about my going to Scotland for a month to try out new sweets and cakes for the Drummonds near Roslyn and to finish writing my cook book.

"Before you go," my love had said. "I want the most complicated sweet thing."

"I can teach you," I'd said, for he was at the door by then: showered and gelled and smelling of Davidoff's Cool Water.

"We'll make it together," he'd said.

"I'll give the instructions," I'd said, kissing him goodbye. "And maybe help out a bit."

Which is what I'm doing by chopping the cherries, so finely that in the sunlight they look like a mound of jelly on the wooden board, their artificial colours bleeding into the grooves. I stand at my love's side and hand them to him to slide into the mixture of sugar, butter, and coconut, then I reach in front of him to turn off the flame.

"Now what?" he says.

"This," I say, holding up the egg.

"There was this cook," he says, and tells me about the chef in the restaurant in Covent Garden where he'd worked who cracked the eggs with one hand.

"Like this?" I say, breaking the egg on the side of a bowl.

My love smiles.

"Show off," he says, and takes the shells from me to throw in the bin.

"I punctured the yolk though," I say.

The yellow creeps out of itself, slow motion into the albumen. And that speck of blood, that sign of life which makes the egg unkosher, that hint of transgression as I watch my love slide the egg from the bowl into the saucepan, the atavistic thrill of it, like eating croque monsieur in Paris for the first time or having a full English breakfast: bacon, pig sausage, black pudding, the lot, while my ancestors do somersaults in their graves.

"Is this what it's supposed to look like?" he says.

"I missed you when I was away," I say.

"Well," he says. "You'll have to aim better next time."

And so I bring the tray back from the fridge where the chocolate has hardened, onto the work surface for my love to spread the coconut on top, and then to return the tray to the oven.

Now the fudge-making can begin.

This is the true act of creation, when soft becomes hard, when sweet things are boiled, then cooled to harden and take shape, become sliceable, each piece distinguished from the next.

"How long have we been together?" I say.

"Months," he says.

"A year," I say.

"Time flies," he says.

"It was a Sunday," I say. "I'd just got back from Durham. Are you listening?"

"Of course I am," he says. "I always listen. You're the one who's always going away."

"I remember buying a pint of milk from the shop opposite the station," I say. "I like that image of me walking across Finsbury Park Station - the place deserted, everyone still asleep - and there I was with my carton of milk about to meet a new man. The chronicles will refer to it as the Sunday of the Milk Carton."

"More like the Sunday of Two Men Fucking," he says.

"Cynicsm is the last vestige of the romantic," I say.

"And what'll happen when your romanticism wears off?" my love says.

"It won't," I say. "As long as you keep looking at me."

My love is the parameters of my story; he is its walls and loving arms. Every moment with him expands into a world of potential, a future, a space much vaster than the past: that gluttonous region that feeds on loneliness. Love would sustain me if I could hold onto it when my love is away from my body. Now I am greedy for more. Now I have to find things to teach my love to keep him at my side, like chocolate coconut fudge bars. My love watches as I put the golden syrup, the butter, the sugar, and the condensed milk into the saucepan.

"Are you ready to begin?" I say.

"I missed you," he says. "You were away for so long."

"It was just a week," I say.

"Tell me how you got to Yorkshire, then," he says, for the stirring must never stop.

And despite my fear of boring him, the fear that the stories I feed him will stop being tasty, I give him the details that children revel in when their parents are safely back home. How long did the journey take? Where did you change trains? Why? Did you have tea at the station? In a pot? With milk? Did you pour it yourself? How long was the second part of the journey? Why? Why? Why? Love can bear these minute details, the way Apollodorus' companion grills him on their way into town: Just one question giving birth to the entire *Symposium*. I, on the other hand, give answers with such caution you'd think I had secrets to keep.

"I wanted you here last night," I say.

The secret is this: I want to know the mechanics of your

breathing; what goes through your mind when you wait for the bus, the train, the washing machine cycle to finish. I want to know what your skin smells like when you wake up, what it tastes like when you're feverish, when you come home from the gym where you've been working out for the past ten years to create the body that stands before me in an apron, in the kitchen, learning how to make fudge.

"I wanted to kiss you goodnight," I say.

"Where?" he says. "On my bottom?"

"No," I say. "On each eyelid."

Slowly. To teach a beautiful man beautiful things. Pause. Go back to the beginning, to that moment you first heard sandalled feet running, crunching on gravel behind you. Wait up, the voice says, tell us your version of the version you heard. So you do your best to impress your good-looking companion, a young, bright academic about to be converted to the literary way of life, a life of back-to-back metaphors. This is the pace to aim for, a slow amble along the dirt road into town, telling stories to the one who loves you.

"The smell of coconut reminds me of tea parties," he says.

When my love was a boy. (Because that's who this story is about. And where does it take place?) On the shores of an ocean, on the banks of a river, at the foot of a mountain as flat as a table. And they were poor. Not long after his father convinced the world he was white, he left the family and went to sell ostrich feathers in the Karoo. My love's mother, too grief-stricken to take care of her children, sent them all - my love and his three sisters - to live with friends near Cape Town. Just for a while, she said. But as so often happens when Time is left open-ended, they landed up staying for years, maybe three, maybe thirty, maybe three hundred.

The friends, a man and a woman whose brothers and sisters had been burnt in a war, were evil. They fed my love chunks of fat, except on the days his mother came to visit. So my love, a boy of seven, starved himself for three days, or three weeks, or was it three years? And every evening when they called him down for dinner the lamb fat was waiting on his plate. So my love got thinner and thinner, and just before the core of what he is now disappeared, his sisters went to their mother and said: Now. That was when she brought them to London.

And the coconut tea parties? the crowd asks the storyteller.

One Sunday, a Sunday when the evil couple had my love's mother over for a tea party, to show her how well her children were being cared for, they sat in the garden and my love's mother looked at him - long before he was mine, in the years when the world was teaching him treachery - and she said to him: "Who's your real mommy?" And my love, for no other reason than to hurt his mother, ran to the evil woman to place his head in her lap. Again and again and again. Three hundred times.

"That's horrible," I say.

"I know," my love says. "But I'm over it."

"Are you?" I say.

"Stop analysing me," my love says.

"Is that what I'm doing?" I say.

Stories told offhandedly, like dreams people give us along with the burden of interpretation, leaving it to us, the lovers of the world, the mad ones, the ones who listen, leaving it to us to tell the full tale. It is those who are left behind who take responsibility for the recounting; whether daily, like me, or like my father whose wife left him with a note on the fridge to say she'd taken my sister and wasn't coming back, or like my friend Dennis whose boyfriend died of lymphoma in their bed. What I keep from my love is this: My great-grandfather left thirteen children to go off and die in Palestine; my grandmother was given to her neighbours in Humansdorp to be brought up as their daughter; my father was sent to live with his cousins when my grandfather drank the money he earned; I haven't been home in twenty-five years. Leaving is our family story.

The table cleared of ingredients, just our mugs of tea now and our chocolate coconut fudge bars before us in a lapis lazuli bowl, sitting here with a sense of triumph and anxiety, ready to feast on a dish of our own creation. The sky has clouded over since morning and the forecast predicts rain. The air is much cooler now as I get up to switch on the lights.

"I was surprised you never called or e-mailed me yesterday," I say.

"Surprised?" he says.

"Yes," I say.

"Why are you saying this just as I'm about to go?" he says.

"It's like therapy," I say. "The important things get said at the end."

The chocolate coconut fudge bars are perfect.

"Is that all?" he says. "Surprised?"

"Okay, devastated," I say.

"Don't be stupid," he says.

"I'm not," I say. "I was devastated. I kill you off each time I don't hear from you. I don't have what it takes to keep you alive for more than twenty-four hours after I've waved to you from the front door and you close the gate behind you, and just before you pass the neighbour's lavender bush, you turn and wave, like that, with your elbow close to your body, a private wave, almost like a secret, a wave that wants to be vast, and I feel like I'm standing on the docks and you're on the deck of a ship pulling out of the harbour, balloons and confetti and streamers all over the fucking place, and I want to dive into the harbour waters and swim after you."

"Talking about waving," he says. "I know you don't love me."

"What?"

"You don't," he says. "You're with me because I'm with someone else."

"What are you talking about?"

"Remember that time," he says. "When you and the dykes left me at the gate at Clissold Park? You didn't even turn around to look at me."

"Oh, baby," I say, my hand reaching across the table. "My baby."

We sit there like that, holding hands across the table, massaging each other's fingers. This picture of a tenderness so extreme, an awkward domesticity, two men holding hands at a kitchen table, how desperate it has always made me feel, and now this awful disappointment that's threatening to kill all hope.

"I want to make love to you," I say.

"Love?" he says.

"Yes," I say. "Come with me."

We take our mugs of tea to the bedroom and my love lies back on the bed, unbuttoning his shirt for me. I take a sip from the mug and with the tea still in my mouth, I suck on his nipple, his flesh in my mouth, the tea hot on his skin as he holds my head down on his nipple and says "oh, fuck," which makes me suck harder, and I let the tea trickle from the corner of my mouth to run across his chest, onto his stomach, down the sides of his body.

"More," he says.

And so our lovemaking continues.

And when it's over and we're lying there, my love on top of me, cum kept warm between us, his head inside the crook of my neck, I say, because I have to know, because I'm not the kind of person who lets goodness linger for too long, because then my superego steps in to accuse me of laziness, and besides, I can't live in uncertainty - that terrifying place where outcomes are left in the hands of others. Because of all that, and because I am beginning to question whether distance can really be love's permanent sustenance, I say: "So, tell me, why didn't you call me?"

"I don't know," he says.

"I think you do," I say.

"I couldn't," he says.

"Why?"

"I didn't want to," he says.

"That's better," I say. "Now we're getting somewhere."

"And where's that?" he says.

"I don't know. Honesty?"

"Honesty?" he says.

"Yes, that's what honesty looks like," I say. "One person telling another person the truth."

"Will you be honest with me while you're away in Scotland?" he says.

"Yes," I say. "Of course I will."

"I don't believe you," he says.

But I am. I'm away for a month and it gives me time to think about the reasons to end this relationship. But, but - that tyrant of the self-doubting mind - but when I hear his voice, when he calls to say how much he misses me; when I get a letter from him to say he wants to lie beneath me, have me warm him with the hairs on my chest; when I dream of us in Paris, buying eclairs from the patisserie on rue de Fleuris, just below Alice and Gertrude's old flat, I wonder, towards the end of these twenty-eight days of making desserts for the Drummonds in their Midlothian castle, whether all my thoughts are rationalisations, just ways of bearing his absence in this magical, wooded landscape. Whether everything I do - and this comes to me on a visit to the National Gallery on Princes Street, seeing Achilles and Petroclus, this fresh shock of my love's presence - whether everything I do is a way of escaping the fear of being left without his beauty and his gaze, and the horror of the self-evident truth that he will never be mine.

Sweetheart, if all feeling went away, what would be left? If I stopped missing you and the sadness that you haven't called were to stop. If the joy of feeling your head on my shoulder, and the thrill of standing next to you on the train to Greenwich eating the chocolate-chip cookies we stole from Tesco's on Canary Wharf, and your kaleidoscope of fluid expressions as I make my way into you, if all that were to stop. If I were ever to forget how crucial your love is to me, who will be there to remind me of you? Will you always be the only true witness of our love?

Chocolate Coconut Fudge Bars

The recipe for the chocolate-coconut base came from Beryl Gready, John Gready's mum. John was my flatmate; now he lives in San Diego with KT. The fudge is my gran's. She used to make this fudge and keep it hidden in the cupboard, in the bar-room that smelled of my grandfather's pipe collection, handing it out sparingly, one square at a time, when we went to visit, usually with my cousins from Admiralty Way. I came across the recipe ten years after she died, and the taste immediately took me back to her kitchen.

Chocolate-Coconut Base

Break up and melt 150g dark chocolate at the bottom of a greaseproof-papered baking tray. Ensure that the base is coated evenly, then put the tray in the fridge for the chocolate to harden. In a saucepan, melt 75g butter, stir in 1¼ cup desiccated coconut, ½ cup caster sugar, one third of a cup of glacé cherries, chopped, and 1 small egg, beaten. Spread the mixture onto the chocolate base and bake at gas mark 4 for 25 minutes. This will be cool by the time you've finished making the fudge.

Fudge

In a saucepan melt 6 tablespoons water, 4 tablespoons golden syrup, and 110g butter. When this has melted, add, one cup at a time, 4 cups sugar, and keep stirring. When mixture starts to boil, add two tins condensed milk and boil on slow stove, stirring constantly, for 30 minutes. The fudge should get to the hard-ball stage. Remove from the flame, add vanilla, and beat for a few minutes. Pour onto the chocolate-coconut base and leave to cool. Cut into rectangular chocolate bar shapes.

So Many Mirrors

A Month in Scotland

So Many Mirrors

There doesn't seem to be much chance of peace in Palestine. Two Jewish soldiers are pulled out of the police station in Nablus by the mob and beaten with bricks and steel pipes; someone breaks a window, the panes of glass smash on the bodies of the two soldiers, like cracking hazelnut brittle on a marble surface to make pralines. A mobile phone rings in the soldier's pocket and one of the Palestinians with bloodied hands answers.

It's a woman's voice: "Sasha?"

"Are you looking for your husband?" he says.

"Yes," she says. "Is he there?"

"Yes," he says. "He's dead. I killed him."

* * *

"Do you ever go back?" she says.

"Never," I say.

Everyone dives into the mushroom paté.

"Do you like it?" Lady Drummond wants to know.

"Yes," we all say, a table of grateful guests.

"Good," she says. "Because I don't care for it much."

I wish we'd said grace at the start of the meal.

* * *

A soufflé de frangipane, then after-dinner conversation: The French academic tells us about helium and hot-air balloons and the balloonist whose polyester shirt caught alight. She has another story about two men who were saved when they landed on the third one, who they crushed to death beneath them when their balloon plummeted to the ground.

"People heard them screaming for miles around," she says.

And although every bone in their body was broken, the two survivors never lost consciousness. Then we talk about the difference between novelists and short story writers: the time one needs to tell a story; the amount of space one takes up in the world.

"What would you say a chef is?" Lady Drummond asks.

* * *

We do the Castle Walk, the Drummonds and I, one morning, past the cave, waving to the woman who lives there ("She does look a bit trogloditic," Lady Drummond says), then down the slope like The Three Billy Goats Gruff, and across the river in our undies ("Good for the circulation," Mr Drummond says), little gypsy girls cheering on the opposite bank, coming over to view my frozen penis. I've been promised tea and cake at Rosslyn Castle and I want it now!

Heading back home, we walk along the disassembled railway line, passing a father and his son. The father carries an old steering wheel; his son - a video camera.

* * *

"Watch me," my sister says, standing on her desk, holding open a copy of *Romeo and Juliet*.

I am trying to get some chewing gum out of the carpet.

"Leave it," she says. "Watch me."

Her T-shirt is tight against her breasts. Her long hair is wound around her skull so that when she wakes up in the morning it'll be straight.

"Now, say," she says. "'Romeo, Romeo, wherefore art thou Romeo.'"

And I do, because I'll do anything to stay in her room.

"Is Stevie coming later?" I say, in love with her new boyfriend.

"He's working, stupid," she says. "Now can we please get back to the play, if you don't mind."

* * *

I need more green in my food. It's all beef, then it's pudding.

So I make a melon and champagne granita to eat between courses, and a pistachio parfait for afters.

* * *

Mornings. After a cold night with not enough blankets, and the heating turned off at eight in the evening, I come down to the hearth-room for tea. Please, I think, no conversation yet. But Lady Drummond is up with her muesli and *The Times*.

"Did you see this?" she says, tapping the paper.

Leni Riefenstahl appeared at the Frankfurt Book Fair to promote her new book. She's 98 and protesting that she only worked for Hitler for seven months.

"Is she still alive?" I say.

"Yes," Lady Drummond says. "My sentiments exactly."

* * *

In the dream my father is on loan from death. Sometimes I think my body has forgotten him, and then, on Tuesday as I wander along the Castle Walk where the path runs parallel to the river, the sun is shining through the trees, on leaves yellow and orange, and it is beauty like this that brings me to tears. The sadness that he will never witness such wonder again.

* * *

How does one even begin to find words for all this beauty? The view from my window at 17:25. The well spreading its shadow onto the grass, cast-iron garden chairs painted green, the castle walls in shades of pink, red, and cream, like pig flesh. Trees on the hillside; if only I could distinguish between birch, oak, sycamore, yew, larch, scrub, sitka, beech, elder, cedar, giant fir. Sunshine deepens the green, and there is an abundance of shade. Then I go down to the kitchen to core, peel, and chop apples for a pouding à la Malakoff. (They say a craving for sweet things is the first sign of a sugar intolerance.)

* * *

Lady Drummond reads to us from Chekhov's "Artistry." We talk about the ease with which he tells a story.

"He is so elemental," she says. "So compassionate."

"He's a bit of a foodie, too," I say.

All that bread and cucumber; and the half-eaten salted herring on a dish, garnished with spring onions and parsley. And in "The Darling," which I read later that night in my room, surprised by the parallels between my own life and the self-negating Olga, and wondering whether she's like the writer who finds his voice through his characters, or the lover who is transformed by love into a more exciting and engaged human being, I come across tea from the samovar with currant buns, and for lunch: borscht and roast mutton, or fish on fast days. And the poor man says to his wife: Let's keep walking past their window until they ask us in.

* * *

Today I wake up wanting only essence. Gold and coal and pearls. Hard-earned essence with a history. I drink tea and sit in my armchair by the window. I am sick of autobiography. I am a hamster on a wheel in a cage. You have to fly to write fiction; the ones with clipped wings and wounds keep repeating their stories over and over again. A baby bird doesn't know it will fall flat on its face if it tries to leave the nest. The only story it knows is flight.

* * *

The sublime is to be found in the nobility of the soul; in a noble emotion in the right landscape; in the proper formation of figures of thought and figures of speech; in the creation of a noble diction; and in the total effect, dignified and elevated.

* * *

God created it all, then he created an audience.

* * *

Burping chocolate chestnut bombe. The Drummonds have gone to bed and I am in the drawing room, puffing away with the bellows, trying to get the fire started again, but the flame keeps disappearing back into the wood. I settle down in the oversized armchair like a dog. I am homeless; I have nothing beyond myself to fight for. That is poverty. Still, all definitions of the self must come from within.

* * *

I have never been in a house with so many mirrors. There is no path to the river. Days begin with the sound of a carpet cleaner. Lady Drummond says it's her way of checking that none of her guests have died in the night.

"It's a family tradition," she says.

"I don't like having my bin emptied in the morning," I say. "I can't start every day with no evidence of the day before."

* * *

Language separates chaos from creation, sky from land, birds from beasts, you from me. Language connects the joy and grief in my realm of no-words to you, my love. It's all I have when our bodies aren't touching.

The Murky Waters of Adultery

Cheesecake Thingies

The Murky Waters of Adultery

I knock, then I hear her coming down the stairs - boom boom boom - no qualms about making her presence known. First her silhouette through the frosted glass window, then the door opens (ah, the wonder of knocking and knowing you're expected) and she's standing there, shoulders naked, skin freckled, a thick lime green towel wrapped around her, tucked under her armpits. This is Ruth.

"I'm early," I say.

"Honey pie," she says, on tiptoes to kiss me.

Her lips, her freckles, her eyes that she squints to focus on mine. I've seen pictures of her as a baby, eyes bigger than her brand-new mouth. Perhaps you've seen her before - in the papers, on television, talking about love and art and inspiration - she got that prize for her first book of poems, the ones about the dying muses in the woods near Cricieth. The critics raved. We did a reading together; I made the leek tartlets. This is the house in Finsbury Park where she lives with Melissa; it is my refuge, my place to rest and seek counsel, especially since falling in love after all these years of singlehood and longing.

"I'm still wet," she says.

Closing the door behind me, the smell of cooking and fresh soap, as I follow her up the stairs where she, her solid body a wellspring of desires and lusciousness, goes into her bedroom as I make my way to the kitchen at the end of the passage. I'm here for dinner, bearing dessert. We've been looking forward to this weekend for months; her love is away at a conference in Oxford: Modern Day Cannibalism and the Consequences of Literal Language, my love, as usual on these days of the week, is with Her, the woman who dusts and hoovers while he irons, the woman whose tragedies and money have kept him bound to her, the woman he sleeps with at night in a T-shirt to hide the marks I leave on his skin.

"I'll be with you now," Ruth says, her bedroom door open.

"I need a shower too, I think," I say. "I'm feeling grimy."

"You're never grimy," she says. "You can shower, though, if you want."

"I just like the smell of it," I say. "And the food smells great."

What I really want is to hear the word 'yes' from as many quarters as possible, to be welcomed wherever I go, to have doors, like outstretched arms, opening up to take me in. This kindness of hers, I think, as I put my cheesecake dessert in the fridge and the three figs on a saucer on the counter, this kindness she offers so casually, as if nothing should be withheld from me, as if my wishes should be granted, no questions asked, now more than ever I am overwhelmed by this kindness. Here I am in the kitchen that overlooks Finsbury Park, rusted leaves unplucking themselves from branches, yellow sycamore leaves flat and slippery on the ground, the pavement dark after an early evening downpour, and the pink sunsets and the cold blue sky (oh, the crispness of it all). First a smile, and then I sob; everything is too unexpected: this feeling of home and safety; my love coming into my life; and the resilient, unwavering generosity of my friends. After so many years of hunger my body is weak and trembling; I wasn't brought up to deal with random acts of giving.

"Check on the meat," Ruth calls. "We're having ribs."

Later, in her black satin dress, the one she bought for the prize-giving . in Bangor, the one that flows from her shoulders, and shows off her nipples, in that one, in the dress that reminds me how friendship, too, would fade without sexual attraction, Ruth feeds us asparagus, and spare ribs in a marinade of honey and lemon and olive oil.

"When we're this close," I say. "It makes me think of college and being naked in bed with you, reciting Donne into each other's mouths."

"I had such firm tits then," she said.

"Me too," I say.

"Nor ever chaste," she says, licking oil and lipstick from her lips. "Except (pause) you (pause) ravish (pause) me."

"I never remember things by heart," I say.

"That's why you keep repeating your stories," she says. "And why I'm a poet."

"I read to him yesterday while he slept on my chest."

"Have you been crying again?" she says, shaking an asparagus at me like an index finger, like the chicken bone Hansel stuck through the bars of his cage.

"It's all too much," I say. "All this love and tenderness."

"You make it sound like a terrible thing," she says.

"It is," I say. "I've waited 35 years and now it's about to end."

"Stop it," she says. "Tell me when you're seeing him again?"

"I don't know," I say, arms folded across my chest. "Maybe never."

"When are you seeing him?" she says, for I must be spoken to like a four year old who's hidden the keys.

"Monday," I say.

"See?" she says, tapping three times on the table. "Now eat."

I'm not an easy person to feed. I don't turn up at the dinner table without expectations. I can tell when a dish has been made with love. Offer to feed me and you risk the wrecking powers of my disappointment. I'm so used to feeding myself that the fear of frustrated hunger keeps me from the dinner tables of others. All my friends are confident cooks, they can make fun of my whining, tell me to stop moaning and eat; all my lovers are gluttons, they expect sustenance. I am both, a cook and a glutton.

"The further I get from him the more I remember who I am," I say. "I forgot for a while."

"You have to forget who you are," she says. "There's no other way to fall in love?"

"But I'm scared I'll go back to what I was before I met him."

"You won't," she says. "It's impossible. Love brands you, like poverty; it'll keep nagging at you to come back."

"I hate it when he's not here," I say, but what I really mean is that my love for him grows when he's not here with me.

"Absent lovers make the best company," she says.

"Is he my lover?" I say.

"Of course he is," she says. "Look what your spirit does when he's away."

"It's like that Williams poem we were talking about," I say.

"Yes," she says. "He's your sleeping lover." She wipes gravy with her finger from her plate and licks it off. "The only reason Williams can dance naked in front of the mirror," she says. "Is the sleeping consciousness in the background."

"It protects him," I say. "But what is it? Is that the ghost of the good mother?"

"And," she says. "It's the knowledge that he's managed to slip away from them. The important thing, though, is that he's still in the same house; he hasn't run away."

"Can I get more wine?" I say, finishing off my glass.

"I'd like some, too," she says.

"God," I say. "It's all a bit much."

"I'm glad you're here," she says.

"How do you do it?" I call from the kitchen, taking a bottle from the fridge, which is always full.

"Do what?" she says.

"Live with someone and still have deep thoughts?"

"Don't," she says. "If we start talking about that, I'll start crying."

"When I called him yesterday I was sick and tired of sleeping alone. I said let's just have a siesta together. So he oohed and aahed all over the place and said: Yeah, okay, but what'll we do when I come over?' So I said: 'Nothing.'"

"Good for you," Ruth says.

"Am I being selfish?"

"Selfish?" she says. "It's not selfish to bear someone's presence. It's baby and Katherine all over again. That's why Williams can dance. But only if the door's closed and they're asleep and he knows he's done a good day's work."

"And when they wake up?" I say.

"That's not a question for poets," she says. "All we want is a moment; we don't deal in what ifs."

"Remember when we danced at Heaven?" I say.

"God," she says. "I was so thin then."

"I want to dance like that again," I say. "With my shirt off, drunk and indifferent."

"So what's stopping you?" she says.

"I couldn't," I say. "I'm too old and too hairy and I care too fucking much."

"Oh, please," she says. "Just bring out the pudding?"

"Which one's that?" I say.

"You know which one," she says.

"Your favourite?" I say.

"Yes," she says. "The best pudding."

She'd given me the cook-book for Christmas with little ticks on the contents page, marking the recipes she wanted made for her.

"Have you been cooking for Martin?" she says.

"I'm too hungry to cook for him anymore," I say. "Every time he leaves I go back to starving mode. He's always fucking leaving."

"Have you told him that?" she says. "Tell him how hungry you are."

"Don't be silly," I say. "He'll never come back then."

Ruth eats dessert with a silver spoon.

"This is perfect," she says, wiping the corners of her mouth with her thumb and index finger.

"I want our conversations to go on forever," I say.

"Martin doesn't trust you when you're not with him," she says.

"I'm his mother," I say. "He needs to know where I am. That's why he'll never leave Katherine. She's always there."

"Are you going to leave him?" she says.

"The more I know him the less I want to be with him," I say.

"That month in Scotland has changed you," she says.

We eat the figs I'd bought to feast on with my love. They are cold and sweet. We agree: their insides are a nest of worms, a dissected testicle, the inside walls of an arsehole, and a cunt, she says, all smooth and grainy. The last fig has burst open on its own, the underside cracked. It is the sweetest. It is the colour and texture of blood and syrup and sand.

"I want him to love me," I say.

"He does love you," she says.

"Does he?" I say. "I'm not sure about that."

"Are you worried that he won't *keep* loving you?"

"I'm stuffed," I say. "I just want to lie down."

Ruth laughs at my diversions, my ability to touch on the truth, and then recoil from it as if it were a cobra. She knows how far I can go. She knows my relentlessness is tentative, that its driving force is the defensiveness of anxiety rather than the courage of a knight-hero. I had ignored her love for so long when we were younger, afraid to take it in, as I am now of the love of others, afraid that the desire was, like my mother's when I was a boy, to mould me into something I am not. I'm not that brave when it comes to love and other hard facts. As for Ruth, I admire her daring and her audacity, the impression she gives that the revolution could start with her.

"Stay here," she says. "I don't like being alone when Melissa's away."

"Can we open this out into a bed?" I say.

"I'll make it up for you," she says.

"Just like old times," I say.

"Is it one pillow or two?" she says.

Ruth sits on the edge of my bed in her pyjamas, thick mustard and mauve stripes, and she strokes my hair. I am up to my neck in duvet.

"Can I get a kiss goodnight," I say.

"Close your eyes," she says.

Her lips are soft on my forehead.

I sleep and I dream, and in the morning when I wake up, my eyes still closed, my first thought is that the worst thing would be to wake up paralysed, for the mind to be moving and working and the mouth to be still, the body frozen. How would I tell people what I want? How would I walk, and do my push-ups? I lay there and there was something of the truth in it - in that lying there with my mind alert and my body still asleep, and I moved my fingers and they were wonderful, and I moved my head from side to side on the pillow, each time my ear touching the cool cotton, like a slow motion shaking of my head, coming alive out of nay-saying. How delicious the knowledge that my dream had not come true.

Sunday morning at the café in Finsbury Park. Resting his head on the table, his T-shirt exposing a smooth strip of flesh at the base of his back. So much depends on the amount of skin revealed unknowingly. This is the morning after ecstasy and Perrier, and the man is waiting for his coffee. He looks up, around, at me, the one who can't stop staring at his perfect waist, his torso in a khaki vest, so we smile.

"Hi," I say.

"Hello," he says.

"How you doing?" I say.

"Knackered," he says, rolling his eyes back. "A bit fuzzy round the edges."

By the pond, two men throw a yellow frisbee between them, like a spider threading its web: back and forth; from branch to branch; wall to wall; washing line to apple tree, where the pink and white blossoms have appeared overnight as if it were spring. They clap for each other when the catch is good (ah, the joy of being caught well). There is no wind, and the air, in the middle of winter, is warm. The men have tied their sweatshirts around their waists, the exposed flesh of their arms changing the nature of my gaze from appreciation to lust.

"Rough night?" I say.

"Kinda," he says.

"It's a good place to come down in," I say.

His boyfriend arrives with cappuccinos and a copy of Rousseau's *Confessions* under his arm. Beauty smiles up at his boyfriend, and we introduce ourselves, three gay men at a café by the lake on a late Sunday morning. Mark and Jean-Claude and me. I could run back to Ruth's for left-over cheesecake; take my first steps into the murky waters of adultery. A threesome: three mouths, three cocks, three arseholes, and six hands; the mind boggles at the combinations. That thrill of a potential secret, something to keep from my love, a counterweight to the extent of the adoration I withhold from him. One love emerges as another is lost.

But they have each other, Mark and Jean-Claude, and that world is closed, just beginning, long before the flood, before the snake, before the birth of a need to try out the forbidden. They have no idea how naked they are.

By the time my love calls that evening, I am too far from home to ever begin to go back. Our story has been one of nostalgia, that strange non-feeling born out of romanticism and disillusionment.

"I want to be nearer," my love says.

"Nearer what?" I say.

"Nearer you," he says.

"Did you get much work done today?" I say.

"I planned a house," he says.

My love is an expert on mergers and acquisitions; he is also a frustrated architect.

"A house?" I say.

"It's made of concrete and glass and looks out onto the

sea," he says.

"Can I come and visit you there?" I say.

"I planned it for you," he says.

"Oh," I say, too touched to be touched. Too tired of staying in love with a man who's only a train ride away, but who won't stop going back and forth between here and her.

We agree on the fundamentals: Our favourite room is the kitchen; we both need to look out onto water; all walls must be white. And yet somehow this common ground only accentuates the uselessness of it all.

"I'll need a room to write in," I say, because I can't stop this make-believe.

"That's on the other side of the house," he says. "Looking out onto the trees."

The perfect answer in the middle of nowhere.

Is it enough to meet like secret lovers, once or twice a week, to get together for cake and tea on park benches, to always have the best sex? Now is the time to choose. Do I stay with him and keep settling for this, or do I believe that one day we will be just us? Is it possible to keep this fantasy world going forever?

Cheesecake Thingies

First make the biscuit base with melted butter and crushed oatmeal cookies; or any cookies will do fine. The plainer they are the better; the cheesecake is sweet and tart in a subtle kind of way and needs something subtle to go with it. Digestive biscuits, for example. Press the biscuit-and-butter mix into cup-cakes. This is the crust. Dissolve 3 teaspoons of gelatine in ¾ cups of boiling water, and let it cool while you whisk 250 ml double cream until it peaks. Fold the cream into a tin of condensed milk, and add 250 ml cream cheese, then 6 tablespoons lemon juice. Stir in the gelatine, then pour the mixture onto the crusts. I prefer freezing these thingies, but you can leave them in the fridge for a softer, creamier texture. No baking necessary.

Something Sour

Something Sour

To see you offer your palm to me. To let that sweet gesture linger - one, two, three seconds, a minute, a week - before I take your hand in mine.

I come to you empty-handed, a lead-heavy suitcase with everything I own, passed down fears and invisible blankets. I wish I'd had one nice thing said to me by my ancestors to pass on to you. So I'll bind you to me like Eve before she turns from rib to woman, squeezing from her husband's body like a butterfly. Bound to him for life. You will lick every inch of my skin, and again, until my body is part of the indispensable history of your tongue. You'll drink fluids from every hole and every pore of my body. We will kiss for days, ceaselessly, until your only language is the desire to fasten your lips to mine. I will scrape your tongue with the bristles of my cheeks and the hair around my arsehole, the dead skin on the soles of my feet. You will learn to love me the hard way.

"That's how I was brought up," you say.

"Nourishment turns so quickly to shit," I say. "I can't seem to hold onto love."

"You're full of anger," he says. "I can see it. You scare me sometimes."

If I could slow down my digestion and let love settle in my stomach, dispatch its minerals and vitamins to my vital organs, will it nourish the hunger that turns to anger? And later, when my body has been enriched, when my soul has grown lighter and is able to soar, will I, in the morning, just once, or perhaps even before bed-time, sit on my chamber-pot, its cool rim on my buttocks, to do a well-formed, slow-moving, quiet shit?

"Sometimes I think writing has kept me from flying," I say. "If our fingers are where our wings used to be, then I've bound my wings to the page."

"Where would you have flown to?" you say.

"Around the world," I say. "Down the road, out of this room."

"This is all I can give you," you say. "What more do you want?"

"I want you to call me when I tell you," I say. "Send me e-mails of great longing and passion. Throw gravel-stones at my bedroom window at ungodly hours, pleading to be let in. I will keep you on my doormat, at the side of my bed, on the tip of my tongue, like a pill, to dissolve. I will swallow you, come inside you, hold you for years as your flesh and mine rot into each other. Come now, lie here on your back while I make my way into you. All we have is the skin of my cock against the moist tightness of your arsehole. This is where I can rest. This is where I give everything to you. Then I will go down on all fours to drink from where I've been, rub my face in the juices we've made. I will lick my way up your spine to your cheek, to your lips that open up to take me in."

"Are you mad at me?" you say.

"God," I say. "Can't you see that that question brings a whole new horrible world into existence?"

They've boarded up the Queen's box at the opera to make room for the exiled Jews to sing their laments, each one frozen in a pose of longing and disaster. *Talises* draped over the scaffolding that serves as both desecrated temple and Babylonian court. The theatre, like the stage, is full of pink faces, except for two: the woman with an elaborate weave, and a man in a sheepskin jacket and a denim hat. On the stage: two blonde Babylonian daughters and a Zacharia with a pony tail half-way down his back. If you get close enough, you'll see the multiple piercings in his ears.

"Give me something," I say. "Before you go I want something from you."
　　"Like what?" you say.
　　"Something to hold onto," I say. "I want an object."
　　"Is this some kind of voodoo thing?" you say.
　　"Forget it," I say. "Let's just move on."
　　"I could give you my pen," you say.
　　"Okay," I say.
　　"No," you say, laughing, getting out of bed.

We are all constantly being sent into exile, having the pages torn from our holy books and chucked in our faces. We've all tried on the king's robes and found them fitting. We've all been chained to the scaffolding, awaiting execution, visited only by our true loves. We've all suffered the long exposed weariness of homesickness.

When you get back from peeing, you say: "Do you think we'll still be doing this in a year's time?"
　　"Yes," I say.
　　"Then I'll take you somewhere to see the sunrise," you say. "But you'll have to climb a mountain for four hours to get there."

And the usher who sells me ice-cream, his fingertips brushing gently across my open palm when he hands me my change. And it's because of this, and because the man in the sheepskin jacket is standing behind me, noticing, that later, as we're walking up St Martin's Lane, stopping together at the traffic lights opposite Pret à Manger, that I ask him if he enjoyed *Nabucco*.

"Why not come over tomorrow?" I say to you later that night. "You could prepare your lecture here."

"We tried that once," you say. "It doesn't work. I'll just be thinking about sex."

"But I'll be out of bounds," I say. "Besides, we had sex yesterday, and Wednesday. We're not as manic as we were that Sunday."

"Don't try and persuade me," you say. "You know how easily I give in."

"No, you don't," I say.

"I do," you say.

"So, give in, then," I say.

That's why I fuck you; I want you to give birth to a part of me that has been purified and transformed by your beauty, a beauty that will exist outside of us, a beauty that will be our creation.

I will carve away the skin to expose the form from the matter in which it was imprisoned, as if the soul were the flesh gradually shed of its bones. The mother fed him like a lump of clay; the food she put inside him would create first the boy then the man she desired. Crocodile meat, ostrich steak, kangaroo flesh, quail's eggs, bull's testicles. May they stick in your throat.

Every act of the imagination is a form of anxiety. Every story is a metaphor. If only you'd had wishes I'd have been your genie.

What If

Making Meringues
Bloody Easy Meringues

Making Meringues

I am inside my boyfriend, Martin, his eyes closed, the candles on the bedside table softening the hues of his face and casting shadows from my body onto his, when he says: "Shaun" - for our terms of endearment are not reciprocal - he says: "Shaun, tell me how you made those meringues?"

Our guests have gone home and we're on our bed, my love on his back and me on my knees between his legs. I take a swig from the bottle we've brought into the bedroom, kiss him, and let wine trickle from my mouth into his. My love is referring to the meringue nests that held the strawberries and the ice cream. That perfect combination of textures.

I say: "Get your ingredients out first."

"And then?" he says, caressing my chest with one hand, the other behind his head.

"You're so beautiful," I say.

My love clenches his arse muscles around my cock, grinning, his long black hair spread out on the pillow, his blue eyes unmoving from my face, his succulent lips shining with kisses. And his armpits. God, his armpits. To think this is where the story began.

"You are so beautiful," I say.

"So beautiful," he says. "And you are so drunk."

"Two eggs at room temperature," I say. "A big bowl, and a smaller one, and sugar."

"That's better," he says, taking his hand from my chest, kissing two fingers and putting them back on my lips.

"Now comes the delicate bit," I say.

"Delicate?" he says. "So soon?"

"Separating the eggs," I say.

"Ah, yes," he says, closing his eyes, moving his arse in circles and smiling, the walls of his insides pressing against the head of my cock.

"Crack the first egg on the side of the small bowl. Let the white of the egg slide out. Pass the yolk between the shells until all the white is in the bowl. Make sure the yolk is intact; no specks slipping out with the white."

"And if the yolk breaks?" he says, pulling himself up as I lean forward to put a nipple between his teeth.

"Oh, fuck," I say, holding onto his back, him onto mine, as I push into him as far as I can go.

"Tell me," he says, my nipple still in his mouth. "What if the yolk breaks?"

"The old-fashioned cookbook... the cookbook says... it says... it says the best way to.... the best way to remove bits of... bits of yolk is..: Ow."

"What?" he says, his tongue flicking the tip of my nipple. "What does it say?"

"Wet a soft piece of linen, squeeze it dry, then dab out the bits of yolk."

"Good advice," he says, lying back again. "Tell me more."

"Both egg whites should be in the big bowl by now," I say. "Get the hand whisk and start whisking the whites."

My love smiles at me, brings one leg over, pushes his bum into my groin, and keeps me inside him. We manoeuvre our bodies so I can fuck him from behind. On my knees I can look out the window, which is open to the night, and snow has begun to fall. The sky is lit up by the city's pink-orange and blue-purple light. The snow falls heavily, piling up on the wall at the back of the garden, on the handlebars and seat of the bicycle in the neighbour's yard, and on the passion-flower vine that blocks their garden from ours. Snow lands on the leaves of the bay tree, weightless snow, snow that is lighter than a leaf.

"Whites of egg need to be stiff," I say, stroking his back.

"I love stiff egg whites," he says, turning his head around to be kissed.

I lift the curtain of dark hair from the side of his face and bring my lips around to his. I run my tongue over his gums: strawberries and dry white wine.

"It's so warm inside you," I say, slowing down so as not to come.

"Tell me what happens when the whites get stiff," he says.

"Sweetheart," I say. "Do you really want to know all this?"

"You know I do," he says. "Just keep talking."

"Take half a cup of caster sugar and pour it in, gradually, while whisking the whites."

"Isn't that a lot of sugar for two eggs?" he says.

His shoulders are speckled with freckles. His skin is beach-sand from a distance, his vertebrae a range of windswept dunes. My love's waist is as narrow as perfection; it's like polished driftwood. The snow has stopped and the neighbour's cat is walking along the wall between our yards. And I think: This is what I came to London for; to see snow settling on clay chimneys; to fall in love with a beautiful man; to write stories. This is what I escaped the unrelenting heat and brutality of Palestine for: the exhilaration of snow illumined by the pink-grey light of a city that neither rejects nor accepts. I am awake and in love at two in the morning.

"What did you say?" I say.

"So much sugar," he says.

"You don't have to worry about that," I say, holding on to him from behind, stroking the soft hairs on his chest.

"I want pink meringues," he says.

"With hundreds and thousands?" I say.

"Of course," he says. "Hundreds and hundreds and

pink."

"We'll need red food colouring then," I say, lifting my chest off his back, fucking him slowly from behind.

"We can use blood," he says, doing that circle motion with his bum. "Just two drops; one from me and one from you."

"Oh, sweetheart," I say, almost coming right there and then.

"What's next?" he says, pushing back against me and pulling on his cock, his face in the pillow, his voice muffled.

"Spoon the mixture onto greaseproof paper, flatten the mounds with the back of a spoon, and leave the baking trays in the oven overnight on a low, low temperature."

"And then?" he says.

"Then, while they're turning into meringues," I say, and cup his arsecheeks, and watch my cock going in and out of him.

"I think I'm going to come," he says.

"Oh, fuck," I say.

"Shaun," he says. "My Shaun," he says, and comes.

I do, too, inside him, and I kiss the top of his back, his shoulders, as we lower ourselves onto the bed, easing our legs out behind us. I am on his back now, still inside him, going soft, stroking his cheek and brushing his skin with my lips. I'm hugging hard earth, peering over the edge of a cliff. I have been here forever. As I slip out of him and curl up at his side, our breathing slows down, and he wriggles his head under my arm to nuzzle up against my chest. We are the tadpoles of the yin and yang circle.

"And the yolks?" he says, letting sleep take him. "What do we do with them?"

"We could make a mousse," I say. "Chocolate mousse."

"Oh, my lovely pink meringue," he says, his lips against

my skin, smiling.

"Ah, my sleeping beauty," I say.

And I kiss him good night.

Bloody Easy Meringues

Beat 2 egg whites until they're stiff and dry, then add a ¼ cup of caster sugar, and keep beating till the egg whites stand up in peaks. Then beat in another ¼ cup of caster sugar and ½ teaspoon of vanilla essence and two drops of red food colouring (optional). Put dollops onto a greaseproof-paper lined baking sheet and flatten them with the back of a spoon. Sprinkle with hundreds and thousands, if you like, and bake the meringues in a very low oven, gas mark ¼ (120°C) until they're dry. Serve them separately, or as a nest for strawberries and cream and ice cream, or stick them together with melted chocolate and custard.

Afterword:
The Last of the Brontës

Afterword: The Last of the Brontës

If you were to die and leave me walking around the table, a Charlotte, the last of the Brontës, unloved and unchallenged, I too would succumb to a cold in pregnancy. What's the point of stories when your audience is no longer there?

Lunch first, and then we're getting undressed in the bedroom, him folding his clothes into a neat pile, removing his watch to place on the bedside table. Then he says: "I hope our relationship isn't just about sex."

"Is that what it feels like?" I say, my heart tired.

"No," he says. "I just hope that there's more to it than sex."

"More to it?" I say.

"Yes," he says. "We're always having sex."

"We've walked through every park in this city," I say. "We've been together to the Serpentine and the British Museum; we spent a whole afternoon at the National Gallery. We've sat on a million benches, under a thousand trees, from elm to beech to walnut. We've eaten enough cake to feed a fucking army. That's more than just sex."

"Oh, no, it's not," he says. "That's all foreplay."

also available to order from www.bluechrome.co.uk

Title: 2003 bluechrome anthology
Author: Various
ISBN: 0-9543796-1-6
Pages: 322
Price: £9.99
Release Date: 1st March 2003
Including the work of award winning authors such as Shaun Levin, Sam Hayes, Ronnie Goodyer and Thomas Pinnock, the bluechrome anthology offers a great collection of short stories and poems.

<u>**All profits from the sale of the anthology are to be donated to the Bristol Branch of the MS Society**</u>

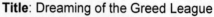

Title: Dreaming of the Greed League
Author: Glynis Wright
ISBN: 0-9543796-0-8
Pages: 502
Price: £19.99
Release Date: 1st January 2003

One fans view of what it means to follow your football team through an extraordinary promotion season

Title: Indigo Dreams
Author: Ronnie Goodyer
ISBN: 0-9543796-2-4
Pages: 248
Price: £7.99
Release Date: 2nd April 2003
bluechrome poetry award winner, Ronnie Goodyer's first collection for the imprint showcases his beautifully lyrical poetry that veers from brutally honest to painfully beguiling. A classic.

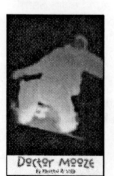

Title: Doctor Mooze
Author: Panton di Villa
ISBN: 0-9543796-4-0
Price: £7.99
Release Date: 30th June 2003

Written by 10-Year-Old Panton di Villa, Doctor Mooze follows a few days in the life of your average English adolescent. A true story that is definitely not one for the kids

Title: Nicolo's Gifts
Author: Neil Ayres
ISBN: 0-9543796-6-7
Price: £7.99
Release Date: 30th June 2003

Nicolo's Gifts is as honest an exploration of the human condition as you are likely to find. Literature, folktales and the constant struggle of the astute mind against the mundane are fused with audacity. Prepare to be enraptured by characters that are as wise as they are naïve and as beatific as they are flawed. Textured and tiered tales at once intriguing and astounding await the adventurous reader. This novel is a genre-blending paradox to delight those of a more exploratory nature

Title: the tsetsefly chronicles
Author: Erik V Ryman
ISBN: 0-9543796-5-9
Price: £12.99
Release Date: 30th September 2003

Perhaps the strangest, most intriguing book ever published in the UK, the tsetsefly chronicles seem destined for cult status, with even the author going *AWOL*

Title	Qty	Price
Indigo Dreams		£7.99
Dreaming of the Greed League		£19.99
Doctor Mooze		£7.99
Nicolo's Gifts		£7.99
the tsetsefly chronicles		£12.99
the bluechrome 2003 anthology		£9.99

To order your copy of any of these fantastic
bluechrome titles you can simply send a cheque to:

bluechrome publishing
38 Tydeman Road
Portishead
Bristol
BS20 7LS

or order on-line at www.bluechrome.co.uk

All cheques to be made payable to "bluechrome publishing" in £Pounds Sterling.
Please add £2.50 per order for Postage and Packing

About Shaun Levin

Shaun Levin's work has been widely published in anthologies as diverse as *Modern South African Short Stories*, *Afterwords: Real Sex from Gay Men's Diaries*, *The Best American Erotica 2002*, and *The Slow Mirror: New Fiction by Jewish Writers*. He lives in London and teaches creative writing.

His website is www.sevensweetthings.com.

Printed in the United Kingdom
by Lightning Source UK Ltd.
9740300001B/16-57